By JOHN TERRY MOORE

Black Dog
The Eleventh Commandment
A Gentle Man
A Nice Normal Family

Published by DREAMSPINNER PRESS
www.dreamspinnerpress.com

JOHN TERRY MOORE

A Gentle Man

Published by

DSP PUBLICATIONS

8219 Woodville Hwy #1245
Woodville, FL 32362 USA
www.dsppublications.com

This is a work of fiction. Names, characters, places, and incidents either are the product of author imagination or are used fictitiously, and any resemblance to actual persons, living or dead, business establishments, events, or locales is entirely coincidental.

A Gentle Man
© 2024 John Terry Moore

Cover Art
© 2024 Reece Notley
reece@vitaenoir.com
Cover content is for illustrative purposes only and any person depicted on the cover is a model.

Trade Paperback ISBN: 978-1-64108-747-6
Digital ISBN: 978-1-64108-746-9
Trade Paperback published June 2024
v. 1.0

Printed in the United States of America
∞
This paper meets the requirements of
ANSI/NISO Z39.48-1992 (Permanence of Paper).

To my husband, Russell.

Acknowledgments

I ACKNOWLEDGE the traditional custodians of the land today and pay my respects to their Elders past and present. I extend that respect to Aboriginal and Torres Strait Islander peoples.

I also acknowledge the people of India, my "cousins" who have emigrated to Australia. Their industrious nature helps keep the wheels of our economy turning and their love of family and friends is inspirational.

John Terry Moore

AUTHOR'S FOREWORD

WELCOME TO *A Gentle Man*.

It combines my love of the Australian country and my connection with South Asia through the maternal side of my family.

The overriding message of *A Gentle Man* is hope.

I share with my publisher the hope that our storytelling not only entertains but influences younger generations, giving them comfort and confidence in a world that is changing rapidly.

Our hope is that LGBTIQA+ people around the world are able to view Australia as a progressive, friendly country with the freedom to be ourselves. That's not to say we don't have our share of religious bigotry, far-right politics, and embedded homophobia.

Our hope is that we assert ourselves, protecting our hard-won rights and privileges, and set an example to younger generations, some of whom struggle with their identity. We hear you; we have been there before you, so listen to our story.

John Terry Moore

JOHN TERRY MOORE

A Gentle Man

CHAPTER 1
MY LIFE AS ME

THE SCHOOL bus lurched along our country "road" as some hopeful dickhead described it, a narrow strip of bitumen broken away at the edges, hardly fit for four-wheel drives, let alone nice cars or even our beat-up old bus. The owner, Clem Smith, was at the wheel today. He reckoned I was ace because I'd replaced the injectors in the big old six-cylinder engine last weekend. I'd explained to him, as a seventeen-nearly-eighteen-year-old farm boy, that he was throwing money out the door because of the fuel he was wasting. Clem's bus could be seen several kilometers away, the billowing clouds of black smoke looking like a bushfire.

Dad had smiled as I turned our big barn at Brookside, our farm, into a workshop, checking the parts first, then getting to work. An hour or so later I had the new injectors installed, bled the air out of the system, and turned the engine over. There was an almost imperceptible puff of smoke; then she settled down to a beautiful purr at idle, like a Rolls-Royce. Clem was amazed and wanted to pay me heaps, but Dad said it was "community service" for the vital link that Clem provided. I pouted a bit, but Dad slipped fifty in my pocket and told me he was proud of me.

"You're so kindhearted, Nick," he said, "such a contrast to your cousins."

I grinned at him; I knew I was like Mum. She's a gentle, lovely lady, proudly Anglo--Indian from Mumbai, an amazing mother to my younger sister, Alexandra, and me. Mum still wore beautiful saris in the summer months, but that wasn't unusual in our area. There were other Indian people in town, several Asian doctors at the hospital, and a large settlement of Sudanese people who had integrated into the community over a long period.

"A far different place to the old days," Dad said, "when the town was very 'ocker,' and unforgiving of anyone who appeared different in any way."

My best friend was Aaron Murphy from next door—the neighboring farm. He and I'd grown up together. Our birthdays were a few days apart.

We were as close as any two blokes could be without rooting each other; the attraction was our friendship. I was gay, he was straight and very possessive, and our families stood around us like a protective shield. We all helped each other—harvesting, shearing, sowing crops—and our fathers held each other upright when they got really pissed, which was quite often.

CHAPTER 2
ALEXANDRA

MY SISTER, Alexandra, has always been amazing. Alex and I bonded as kids mainly because we were so close in age, but we also liked each other. Mum and Dad saw the teamwork and loyalty between us and laughed at us as we raised each other! Under those circumstances, and with Mum and Dad encouraging us, we matured way before our time and were regarded as the "know-alls." Other kids at school would pick on us on a daily basis. Dad suggested we could do with some self-defense training when some of the criticism was beginning to get physical.

A small but clean house in town with a substantial corrugated iron building at the rear was where we trained, owned and run by Mr. Teo, a Thai man and a Taekwondo Grand Master, rare outside the capital cities. Inside, the building lost its sterility with a timber floor and all sorts of machinery which served as a gymnasium. At the rear were mats, and this was where Mr. Teo was truly at home and where we learned the basics of Taekwondo. Alex was a stunning natural. I wasn't, but I enjoyed the lesson so much I decided to invite Aaron along. Ted Murphy, Aaron's dad, wasn't keen, so Alex sprang into action. In a sweet, imploring way, she sold the Murphys the character-building aspects of Taekwondo, and by our second lesson, a bemused Aaron was with us. Aaron was at our place more than his own and always hanging with us, so this wasn't too much of a stretch. We all enjoyed it, but we were the three youngest students by far. Most of the other students were in their late teens onward, with quite a lot of professional people both working out and learning martial arts of some sort as well.

It was around this time I knew I was gay, irrefutably. We'd always been encouraged by our parents to recognize nature in all its forms and variations, and I worked it out for myself. I loved everything about blokes, and I decided to come out to my family, including Aaron and his parents. As far as I was concerned, we were all one family anyway. Aaron and I had been in each other's lives since birth, and Alexandra tried to fill in the void in Aaron's life when his own sister passed away. She was spectacularly successful, Aaron often referring to Alex as "Sis." Both Alex and Aaron were highly protective of me, and while I was mute about anything sexual at school, someone started a rumor because I politely refused an invitation to go out with a girl to the local cinema. Alex was furious. Normally a pleasant, well-spoken young lady, Alex turned into a fishwife when anyone threatened anyone she loved. Aaron was also dangerously quiet, like a volcano on standby.

David Lane was a farmer's son in his final year at high school, a born bully, and it was easy to establish that he was the rumormonger. He was overweight and had halitosis and the personality of a farm gate: "Always open and squeaking," Aaron said.

We got the catcalls as we hopped off the school bus. Lane was leading the chant. "Fag-got, fag-got, fag-got, doesn't like fanny, poofy boy, poof, poof, poofter," they sang.

I was elbowed by one hopeful, impressed by the Lane family's net worth (about five properties), so he thought he'd show allegiance to all that lovely money by getting physical. I quietly lifted him off the ground by grabbing his shirt with one hand. His eyes widened, and he muttered, "I'll get you for that you fuckin' poofter," as Aaron, Alex, and I continued on to class.

The three of us waited behind the shelter shed for five minutes before lunch. We knew it was David Lane and his cronies' favorite place for a cigarette or two out of sight of teachers. As they walked around the corner of the shed, patting their pockets, searching for their cigarettes, Alex spoke up.

"Oh, going to join us in a fag, are we," she taunted, as Lane ran at her.

She stepped to one side deftly and, using his weight to advantage, threw him on his back on the uneven ground. Then she aimed her nice school shoe and kicked him hard in the balls. He screamed, and his cohorts turned to run. Aaron and I shepherded the others into a corner of the shed.

"Now," said Alex with authority, and the guy who'd elbowed me that morning pissed himself, the stain spreading all over the front of his nice pants. "If I hear any one of you fucking retards talking about my brother, or anyone else, for that matter, you'll get a touch of what Mr. Fucking Cunt Face Lane got, understand?"

They all nodded except one who sneered, "Lucky punch."

My fourteen-nearly-fifteen-year-old sister was tall for her age. She stared at him with distaste and quickly stamped hard on one of his feet. He yelped, bending over in pain as she chopped him under the chin with her fists together, hammering his head backward into the weatherboards of the shelter shed. He went pale and began vomiting.

"Oh, poor darling," said Alex, "you must have eaten something that's upset you. And if any of you miserable cunts try wailing to the teachers, Aaron has a recording of your homophobic outburst this morning when we arrived at school. Anyway, who'd believe you'd be so scared of a fourteen-year-old girl? Now fuck off, losers, before we get serious."

CHAPTER 3
LIGHTS AND SIRENS

THERE WERE only about ten of us on the bus that day. Alex was already home, we'd dropped off several kids and were headed toward our properties. Aaron and I sat in the back seats, talking shit as usual but enjoying each other's company. I could hear something in the distance behind us and the noise was becoming louder.

"What's that?" I said.

Aaron cocked his head to one side, listening intently. "Sounds like a siren. Actually, more than one."

We peered out the back window, and sure enough, there were blue and red flashing lights everywhere. Clem pulled off to one side and stopped, allowing a procession of vehicles to speed past in a hail of loose gravel and wailing sirens. First, a white all-wheel drive wagon with MICA—Mobile Intensive Care Ambulance—Paramedic along the side, followed by an ambulance and a police car at the rear. Clem started the bus again and trod on the pedal because we all wanted to know where the emergency vehicles were headed. We swung around the corner and over the bridge at Mulligan's Creek, cresting the rise near our homestead, and my heart dropped like a stone. The convoy of lights and sirens were passing our barn and heading toward the back of our property. I knew already Dad was in trouble, and Aaron held my hand, squeezing it for comfort. We jumped out of the bus together and started running. It was clear nobody was at the house, so I gunned up the old Landcruiser tray at the barn and followed the other vehicles. I could feel the tears coursing down my face as Aaron squeezed my leg, trying hard to be strong for me, but the farther we went, the worse the situation seemed.

Dad had warned me many, many times about the track above the creek, because erosion had weakened its foundation. We'd had rain recently, and I knew it'd be soft and unstable. We crested the rise and saw Mum and Alexandra standing there, arms around each other. My gaze drifted to the right, and I saw the wheels of the quad bike covered in mud but upside down. The paramedics were working patiently but without haste, and being a realist at heart, I guessed it was all over for my father. The MICA fellow went over to Mum and Alex as I pulled up alongside. He introduced himself, and held our hands, explaining Dad had been thrown off but then crushed by the roll bar, the very item designed to keep drivers safe. He asked if we could be understanding while the police took photographs. As soon as that was done, they'd take Dad to the hospital. I cuddled Mum and Alex, and Aaron pushed his way in for a group hug, with tears of desperation. He rang his parents, and within minutes the Murphys arrived as the paramedics extricated Dad from the wreckage. They straightened him up, cleaning some of the mud off him as Mum watched on. A wail of anguish arose from my mother as she gripped one of his lifeless hands, echoing her grief, eventually stumbling backward into Mrs. Murphy's arms. Alex and I were swept up by Aaron, who drove the Landcruiser, followed by Ted and Bernice Murphy with Mum in their four-wheel drive.

The ambulance crept along, followed by the other vehicles, a sad, sorry procession. They hesitated at the gate while Geoff, the MICA bloke, got out and asked Mum if she wanted another viewing. Mum shook her head, and he waved the ambulance on. It quietly turned onto the road and within minutes had vanished from sight.

Tony Fennell, the police sergeant, was also mindful, telling us he'd be back for a statement when Mum was feeling better, and she smiled a wan smile of gratitude. To my surprise Geoff, the MICA man, had put the kettle on, and he sat with us around the table, talking quietly to Mum. From being nearly catatonic, Mum had relaxed somewhat and sipped her tea. A tap at the door and our GP, Graham Deacon, entered and kissed Mum on the cheek, prompting another waterfall of tears. Mrs. Murphy helped Mum shower, and only then did Graham administer a shot to help her sleep. Alex and I went in and held her hands as she drifted off, fighting it a little but giving in to healing sleep before all the shit began again the next day.

CHAPTER 4
A WAITING GAME

MY EIGHTEENTH birthday had come and gone while we waited on the coroner. I felt a terrible numbness, as I guess Mum and Alex did as well. The world as we knew it had stopped still. Everything around us reminded us of Dad. We'd sniffle a bit and then get on with what we were doing. Rusty, Dad's kelpie, was inconsolable. He was the last living thing to see Dad alive, but he still thought Dad would appear from behind the barn and kept watching for him. We sometimes forget how smart animals can be and found ourselves helping this beautiful creature deal with his loss, which seemed to help us do the same.

We all looked out for each other, I talked to Alex a lot about what life would mean without Dad, and she nodded, internalizing everything. Mrs. Murphy spent most of her time at Mum's side, and Aaron slept with me every night, making sure I felt loved and respected. One day melted into another, but what helped keep me going was the farm. There was always work to be done, and Alex made sure she was around to help. She was only eighteen months younger than me, and at sixteen and a half she was already a smart and mature young person. She knew her way around the farm chores, feeding the chooks, even mowing the lawn around the homestead, quietly nursing her grief but reaching out to Mum and me from time to time. The three of us were in this together, and we thought we were doing well until Uncle Robert, Dad's brother, arrived.

He'd been in Sydney, on church business, and couldn't come home after the accident until three days later because he was "involved in the work of God"—a national conference of church elders.

"I'm so sorry, Sophia," he said to Mum as he stormed in the kitchen door, "All full of piss and importance" as Aaron whispered.

"Who are you," he snapped at Aaron.

"I'm Aaron Murphy," he said, "from next door."

"Thank you, we have private family business. Please leave."

"Aaron stays here with us," I said, and both Mum and Alex nodded their agreement.

"You don't have any authority, child, and a creature of your persuasion should be hidden from sight at a time like this."

Mum's eyes widened in shock and anger; I'd never seen her in a state of such cold determination, ever. "Robert," she said in a measured tone, so it was obvious to anyone with a smidgeon of common sense she was offended. "Nicholas is now eighteen years of age, so his authority, as you put it, is recognized by the government of Australia. I take it your other remarks are in reference to Nick's sexuality, which is both none of your business and highly offensive."

"I agree," Aaron said. "Not very Christian, Robbie boy. How would you like to hear some stories about your kids? We could keep you entertained for hours. Perhaps you'd better piss off while you're in front."

Mum, I knew, would probably ask for the stories about our cousins later and laugh at Uncle Robert's discomfort, but she had a parting shot. "Aaron is as much a member of our family as we are of his. We can always rely on the Murphy family in times of need, unlike the Williams family, too busy with God and Jesus to do the Christian thing and return home immediately with practical help, comfort, and love."

The color drained from Uncle Robert's face as he faced the challenge across the kitchen table. "B-b-but," he stammered, "I have to organize the funeral. I am the executor of the estate, after all."

"It's all been done, with help from Nick, Alexandra, Aaron, and his family, thank you. Three o'clock next Wednesday afternoon, with a private cremation to follow."

"But there's been no booking made at the church. I checked."

"Oh, that would be because it's being held in the funeral home's chapel, with a civil celebrant."

"But you must have it in the church. The Williams family has always been Christian. This is dreadful. Awful."

I couldn't stand the bullshit anymore, but I tried to stick to the facts and fuck off Uncle Robert so we could relax for the evening. "Uncle," I said, "Dad had a codicil added to his funeral instructions about two years ago. He'd had a gutful of the hypocrisy of Christianity about the same time as Mum stopped practicing her faith. So, if you've finished, we'd like to eat. I'm starving. Perhaps you'd like to break bread with us after your long trip."

"No," he said.

"Fine, we'll see you on Wednesday."

CHAPTER 5
A HAPPY FUNERAL

DAVID CANNING had married Mum and Dad around twenty years ago and had remained a close friend of the family. He was originally a country person and loved visiting with his husband, Peter. He and Dad, together with Ted Murphy, had a liking for red wine, and their "soirees" in the barn were infamous for their carousing and sore heads the following day. When it came to country matters, the thirty-odd years between Dad and David disappeared instantly; they were like two little boys playing with their toys and talking about all things agricultural. I can remember David on our tractor, baling hay while Peter cooked up a storm in the kitchen. They'd often stay a few days, help us out at harvest time, then return home.

Although in retirement the old fellow didn't hesitate to help, sharing our grief with his own. When he and Peter returned, the night before the funeral, he read the ceremony for our approval, and we didn't change a word. He took Mum's hand and spoke gently to us around the kitchen table. "You know, we can't do anything more for Trevor other than give him a faithful and respectful farewell tomorrow." We all nodded like little dolls in a row.

"If I could bring him back, I would, but I can't. The people I have to concentrate on are you guys, including you, Aaron. You were like another son to him," he said, "and also your mum and dad. You were all part of his family group, the one that mattered at least. You see, life goes on, and we have to do what your dad would expect us to do—get on with it, move on with our lives while we remember him and his contribution."

Ted and Bernice Murphy walked in the door, Ted with not one but three bottles of red wine while Bernice brought even more food, the way country people demonstrate support for each other. David talked about a day of celebration tomorrow, not a day of mourning, reminding everyone that's exactly what Dad would have wanted.

THE HEARSE circled the barn, as planned, coming to a halt at the garden gate, followed by a stretch limousine. The limo door swung open, and we piled inside with the Murphy family. Uncle Robert, Aunt Anne, and our cousins filled the following two vehicles, while David and Peter Canning rode with us.

As we made our way toward town, there were vehicles waiting at farm gates to join the procession. Aaron's eyes grew huge, as I suppose mine did. There must have been well more than a hundred vehicles now following the hearse.

Regardless of David Canning's advice, I felt intimidated. The chapel was packed with people, many of whom I'd never even met before, most sitting, some standing at the rear and outside where I could see a large television screen relaying the service. I sat up front with Mum and Alex plus the Murphy family. I was so proud of Mum. She was dignified yet welcoming to everyone, making sure her gratitude for the messages and gifts over the last ten days weren't overshadowed by her grief. She squeezed my hand, then did the same to Alex. We'd get through this and move on. Aaron reached across and kissed Mum's hand; he was, as usual, on the same wavelength! Ted and Bernice were right there with us. Grief was no stranger to them; they'd lost their three-year-old daughter to a rare form of leukemia some years ago. After Bernice suffered a series of miscarriages, they stopped trying, and Aaron became an only child. We all understood why Bernice and Ted encouraged Aaron to spend time with us. The truth was he didn't need much encouragement!

Across the aisle sat Uncle Robert and Auntie Anne with our four cousins. "Look at the brains trust," Aaron whispered. It was a perfect description, and we all lightened up.

Uncle Robert had a pained expression on his face, clearly not happy with the absence of religious fervor at his brother's funeral. Aunt Bitchface, as we called her, was even more devout than her husband, and her disapproval was registered in her facial expression. Her nostrils flared on her pointy nose rather like she'd let some gas go and was smelling her own farts.

Richard, their eldest at sixteen years of age, was a chronic masturbator. He shuffled in his seat; it was obvious something was turning him on, as the lump in his trousers wasn't going away, and he was looking around desperately trying to find something or someone to wank over. Amanda, the next eldest, was well-known to most of the male population of the district. At only fifteen years of age, she'd seduced football teams, the Angler's Club, even had an up-righter in the church vestry, without her parent's knowledge of course. Then there was Danny at thirteen and Gillian, twelve, who seemed almost normal compared to their older siblings.

The music was light, some of Dad's favorite old-fashioned musical-theater tunes. He had a liking for Gilbert and Sullivan, which he shared with David when they were rotten as chops at the bar over in the barn. No dirge- like church music, which can make people weep in the first stanza. We understood David's strategy; he'd explained people often felt such simple unnecessary guilt when a tragedy happened. Things like not catching up for a long period, a disagreement of some sort, and all the "what if?" scenarios. He fixed that in a few sentences, and I marveled as I watched the old bloke settle everyone down around us. Shoulders relaxed as the tensions ebbed away and a few smiles appeared. Uncle Robert and Aunt Anne sat there like a pair of stunned mullets, clearly their first experience of this type of service. Mum stirred and smiled at me; she felt the positivity in the room. Aaron did also. The guy was so smart. He gave everyone the impression he was the village idiot, but I knew differently.

The mood shifted as David presented "The Man in the Mirror," a reading which sounded so like Dad. Then came the eulogy, the story of Dad's life, peppered with as much humor as possible to keep the air of celebration going, defying sadness at all costs. Peter joined his husband at the podium as they spoke jointly of the wonderful times they'd shared with our family, but with a focus on the future, emphasizing that Dad would expect there were many more wonderful times ahead, regardless of his absence. Then it was my turn, with Alex, as we stood together at the podium. We knew the message was simple and clear and important to the end result. Uncle Robert had declined to speak, so we had the floor and presented a simple little poem by Mary Lee Hall we'd found:

> If I should die and leave you here awhile,
> Be not like others, sore undone, who keep
> Long vigils by the silent dust and weep.
>
> For my sake turn again to life and smile,
> Nerving thy heart and trembling hand to do
> Something to comfort other hearts than thine.
>
> Complete those dear unfinished tasks of mine
> And I, perchance, may therein comfort you.

Then David did the committal. He reminded everyone that, through genetics, Dad actually lived on through me and Alex. So he was still around, because he was part of us. As long as we were here, Dad was still here.

"I am the Very Model of a Modern Major General" rang out, completely irrelevant to the proceedings, but Dad had loved it, and it made people happy. As people were asked to stand, they smiled, cried, and laughed. People said afterward it was the first funeral they'd attended where guests applauded the deceased as he left the chapel. They danced along, some singing the lyrics, as we wheeled Dad to the waiting hearse. It was over. Dad would have loved it with everyone feeling positive, calm, and relaxed. I felt arms slip around me with a chin in the crook of my shoulder, Aaron protecting and calming me, and I knew Dad would approve.

CHAPTER 6
THE DAY AFTER

I HAD a mixture of tasks ahead of me. Nearly two weeks had elapsed since Dad's passing, and I needed to complete my projects and submissions necessary to qualify for my Leaving Certificate. But there were about a hundred and twenty late fat lambs that had scoured badly and needed crutching before they went to the local sale yards. Importantly, they didn't need to lose any condition, so I'd been feeding them some oats to keep them going, in a dry paddock.

I was having breakfast with Mum and Alex when a green Mazda wagon drove up to the back gate. I rolled my eyes. Please, not more stuff to handle when I had so much to do! There was a knock, and in walked Mr. McPherson, one of the teachers from school.

"Thought you could do with a hand, Nick," he said. "We should be able to knock most of this stuff off today, and then you can concentrate on your farm work."

I was flabbergasted; surprise number one for the day! Mum made him coffee, and we set to in the dining room. Much of the stuff was oral in nature, so we covered ground quickly. My phone rang, and I excused myself. It was Ted Murphy.

"Aaron and I will help you crutch the lambs tomorrow," he said. "Just have a nice rest tonight, mate."

Before breakfast on Saturday morning, I took Rusty, and we drove the lambs to our little shearing shed, penning them under cover. Rusty now shadowed me; he'd almost given up looking for Dad, but he understood who the new boss was, always looking for directions.

I was finishing breakfast when Aaron and Ted arrived. I knew, even at this early stage of life without my father, that I had to plan everything better going forward and realized the combs and cutters hadn't been ground and sharpened, let alone had I even checked the handpieces. As if he were reading my mind, Aaron had theirs on two pieces of fencing wire, which he rattled at me. "Come on, bitch," he said pointing to the shearing shed. "I guessed you wouldn't have time to get set up, so we'll use ours."

"Thanks," I mumbled, and he kissed me on the cheek with Ted and Mum watching and smiling. That was my mate—such a thoughtful and caring human being I sometimes had to pinch myself that I could be so lucky to have a friend as amazing as he was.

CHAPTER 7
A CAREER BY DEFAULT

MUM AND I sat at the dining table surrounded by paper. The details of Dad's last will and testament were straightforward enough—everything was left to Mum as expected, with Uncle Robert to provide "administrative assistance" as executor. What Uncle Robert didn't know was that Mum had also been named as an executor, so in fact his presence was more of a nuisance than a benefit.

Thanks to Mum and Dad's management, we only had a small mortgage remaining on the property; and they'd managed to trade overdraft—free for the last two seasons. Ever since we were tiny little kids, Alex and I were included in our parents' financial affairs, quite deliberately. We could read a balance sheet at ten and nine years of age respectively and were surprised that our fellow students at school had no idea what running a set of books entailed.

Today, Mum was reminiscing. "I was in my final year of accounting at the university when I met your dad," she said. "I was introduced to this handsome Australian student studying agricultural economics, and it was love at first sight." She smiled, almost to herself, remembering, pushing away her grief in favor of pleasant memories. "But we have to get on with it, Nick," she said. "Dad would expect us to manage our assets and dispose of them as we see fit."

"Dispose?"

"Yes, dear, that has to be our priority, but we have to stay as profitable as we can until everything is sold."

"Mum," I snapped, "there's no need to sell the farm. You know bloody well I can run it with my eyes shut, even in a crook season, and we're having a good one now, except for Dad of course." I sniffed, Mum did the same, and we laughed at each other. "What are you winding me up for?" I asked.

"I need to know if this is what you want from life, Nick. Once you commit yourself to this place, your career choices are limited. I'd hoped you'd go to university, maybe do law or economics—you're strong in both arts and science subjects, which is unusual—move on to a profession that doesn't have the inherent risks of poor seasons, natural disasters, fluctuating markets, and worse, fluctuating prices."

I looked at her with fondness. "Mum, I want to be a farmer, period. I want to be in a business partnership with you and Alex. For the next while, however, I want to work part-time for Mr. Fleming at Evergreen Machinery and attend night school, so I have diesel technician qualifications as a backup, just in case everything goes to hell in a handbasket. You never know what's around the corner."

"Talking about what's round the corner, here comes your Uncle Robert," Mum said. "Okay, let's stick to our strategy."

Uncle Robert strode into the room in his normal manner, and with his normal lack of manners. "Sophia how are you?" he said in his best Sunday voice.

"We're actually doing quite well, thank you, Robert. Much better than anyone expected."

Before Uncle Robert had a chance to further ignore me, I said in a well-modulated and very firm voice, "And I'm also very well indeed, thank you, Uncle Robert. Much better than you expected I might be and thank you for asking! I was watching your face during Dad's service, and I actually thought you looked pleased that Dad was getting exactly what he wanted, a happy funeral."

The look of sheer enjoyment on my mother's face gave way to a more somber expression as Uncle Robert snarled at me. "I don't acknowledge rudeness, particularly coming from the younger generations, and particularly from you as a degenerate. Sophia," he said, "might I have some private time with you?"

"Of course, Robert, as long as Nick is present."

"What I have to say has nothing to do with him."

"It has everything to do with Nick," Mum said. "The partnership agreement between us has been drawn up and simply awaits our signature," she lied. "When Alexandra turns eighteen next year, she will also be included, at Nick's request."

"But the property must be sold as soon as possible, and such a partnership would only complicate matters."

"The property isn't for sale, Robert." Mum smiled. "We're having a wonderful season, and there's no reason to sell at the moment."

"But I've listed the property for sale with Richards and Company in my role as executor."

"Then, Robert, you should get it unlisted as quickly as possible, because I'm also an executor, and a sale is out of the question."

"I've seen no evidence of that."

"What date is your copy of Dad's will?" I asked helpfully.

Uncle Robert looked at me with pure hatred in his eyes. He glanced downward, sighed, and said, "October 3, 2014."

"Aah, the later one with the nonreligious codicil was January 13, 2016. That's when Mum was also made an executor." I smiled.

"We'll call you, Robert, if we need assistance," Mum said. "We do appreciate your concern."

"Well, if you want to sell this place, I'd take it off your hands to help you out."

"That's very Christian of you, Uncle Robert," I said as he turned and stomped out the door.

CHAPTER 8
A FARMER'S LIFE

AT NEARLY two years since Dad's passing, I think there was an element of surprise from neighbors and friends at how well we were managing. Brookside was almost totally flat country with good deep volcanic soil, and after talking with Mum and Alex, I approached a new company setting up on our side of town to process canola oil. I'd grown a trial plot in the vegetable garden, read up on everything, and was ready to go. Except we'd have to make an upfront investment of around two hundred thousand dollars in equipment.

Then they gave us an offer we simply couldn't refuse—we could lease a seed drill and harvester for the season, then evaluate the program post-harvest. Hopefully our experience would lead to other growers joining up.

I sowed the crop in dry ground, and as I backed the drill into the barn, it began to rain. Perfect timing—the autumn break arrived with constant gentle rain on warm ground. Within days there was an even strike, a green carpet from one fence to the other. If this worked and the income was right, cropping would form part of Brookside's income permanently, and we could reduce our reliance on beef, fat lambs, and wool.

ALEX AND I made sure Mum had a night out once a week. Sometimes Aaron came along, and sometimes Ted and Bernice, or Bernie as she was known to the family. We'd have a nice meal, maybe play the pokies, breaking the monotony of farm life. Mum had friends in Geelong, Victoria's largest regional center, only an hour away. We encouraged her to drive up, even spend the night and relax with her mates, several of whom came from Mumbai, her birthplace.

Friday and Saturday nights Aaron and I would go into town, usually to one of the pubs where there was some music.

"Not much around for you tonight," I said to Aaron.

"Jesus," he said, "look at those two heifers over there. I reckon you'd turn straight for them."

"You've got to be joking, Joyce. They're your type of love interest, not mine."

"I'll bet their old man's a dairy farmer," Aaron whispered. "They've come straight from the shed after the second milking. They're fuckin' gigantic!"

"Well, they're certainly very healthy. Probably really nice chicks. You should go over and chat them up."

He grinned at me, but did the nice and gentlemanly thing, walking over to the girls and introducing himself. Unlike most blokes who would have hit on them immediately.

"Nick, come over," he bellowed to me, and I walked across. "This is Jasmine and Ebony," he said smiling. "I said you were out, and they should do the same thing. This town isn't as straitlaced as it once was, and they shouldn't have to hide their love affair anymore."

"How did you know," Jasmine said.

"Nick is my social barometer."

"I simply said you looked like nice girls and that he should say hello," I replied.

Up to this point in time Jasmine had been the spokesperson, but Ebony took over. "It might have been the withering look I gave him," she said. "I saw him walking across and thought, *Not another prick after a quick root,* and put my arm around you, and I think Aaron noticed."

"You got it in one," Aaron said, slipping his arm around my shoulder, "got to look after our mates."

CHAPTER 9
MELBOURNE

"YOU GOT a clear weekend?" Aaron asked.

"Yes, but I can't stand going to the pub or a club again. There's no social life for a gay boy down here."

"What about your sex life?"

"There's plenty of that, but it's all boring. It's almost always on the down-low so their missus or girlfriend doesn't twig. I'd love to meet someone I can actually *talk* to."

Aaron laughed; his distinctive, infectious laugh identified him anywhere. "You don't have to fall in love with 'em, poke 'em and move on, mate."

"But that's the problem. I wouldn't mind a boyfriend, but even though my sexuality was accepted at high school, no bastard would dare walk hand in hand with me down High Street."

"I would," Aaron declared, "and they could all get fucked."

We looked at each other and roared with mad laughter.

"Including Uncle Robert?" I asked.

"Including Uncle Robert."

WE DECIDED to catch the train to Melbourne on Friday night. It was only a little over two hours. We'd stay two nights and come home on Sunday. We found a nice little holiday rental apartment at a good price in Prahran, quite near the gay district.

"What are you going to do with yourself?" I said to Aaron as we unpacked and made ourselves comfortable.

"I'll tag along with you mate, if you don't mind, but tell me if I cramp your style."

"That's fine, but the likelihood of you finding a bed companion in gay bars and restaurants is a bit remote."

"Nah, can't be bothered, I feel like you. I'd like someone sensible to talk to for a change, and gay people seem to be quite interesting, mate."

"But I'm the only gay person you know."

"Well, you're interesting."

"Gee, thanks."

His bloody eyes laughed at me again, and I thought I had to keep my feelings for my straight mate locked away, out of sight and hearing. We had an amazing friendship, and I didn't want to fuck it up by making a play for him because I knew I'd lose him, and I couldn't handle that. As we'd grown older, our friendship had deepened, and I felt myself depending on him, increasingly. His opinion mattered to me, and vice versa. I could see myself heading toward a broken heart, yet he was like a drug, I couldn't give him up. He was there, all the time in my life, and I had to deal with it.

WE FOUND a restaurant nearby in Chapel Street and ordered up on seafood, which we both loved.

"Jesus this is a good feed, don'tcha reckon," Aaron said, stuffing his face with calamari. I nodded, my mouth full as well. The meal was expensive, and our waiter hovered around us like a drone on a military mission.

"We'll have another bottle of the pinot grigio, thanks," I said.

"Yes sir," he replied, affirming our order with a patronizing look in his eyes, then scuttling away toward the bar.

It hit me at the same time as Aaron. "He thinks we're country bumpkins because we're probably not up with the local dress code, doesn't he?"

"Yes, I never gave any thought to our clobber," I said, feeling a touch defensive. "But fuck it, our money's as good as anyone else's, and there's nothing wrong with the way we're dressed."

My mate stared into the middle distance. "Makes you wonder why we bothered," he said. "Are you on Grindr?"

"Yes, and you'd have to be on Tinder or similar."

"So does Grindr work for you?"

"As I made the point before, the so-called straight married ones are always lurking around, always on the down-low, plus the occasional visiting sales rep in town. And that's why we're here. What about you?"

"Only old aunties and huge sheilas like Friesian heifers."

We roared with laughter as our waiter returned with our wine. He sniffed as he refilled our glasses and proceeded to drive the bottle with some force into its bed of crushed ice in the silver bucket.

"What's wrong mate?" Aaron said. "You look like you need a good shit. Aren't we social enough for you?"

"My dears," a loud voice rang out, "the question is, are *we* worthy of your lovely business?" A huge, tall drag queen strode up to our table.

"I apologize for the waiter's rudeness," she went on, smiling, while Aaron looked on, speechless for once. "I'm sick to death of pretentious queens. This is his last night anyway. My name is Hyper, and I own this place." She clicked her fingers, and a young girl appeared with a tray and two glasses. "Here's two Drambuie's by way of apology."

She reached into a smart-looking valise and searched for a moment. "This isn't my only job." She smiled sweetly. "I run the drag show just up the street. This will get you in. No charge."

CHAPTER 10
DRAG QUEENS GALORE

"OH, FRIENDS of Hyper," said the doorman, a youngish and very attractive Indian guy, as we handed in our tickets.

"Hyper?" said Aaron, still not believing his ears.

"Yes, Hyper Ventilating. Easy to remember."

Since we'd had two bottles of wine and several liqueurs, we giggled and giggled, the doorman doing the same. "I'll catch you inside later," he said and winked at me. Out of the corner of my eye I saw Aaron's face darken, and I thought, *I'd better watch myself. No one will be good enough to pass muster because my lovely straight mate is in protector mode.*

It was early in the night, although for country people it was nearly bedtime! But the band was rocking, and my big mate pushed me onto the dance floor. We invented our moves, which were clearly agricultural, but only the odd punter noticed. We didn't care anyway. It was clear Aaron was enjoying himself, and the twinks made a beeline for him. We were having a refreshing beer at the bar when one of them sidled up, grabbed him around the neck, and kissed him. He must have been ambidextrous, because he managed to cop a good feel at the same time. Aaron gently but firmly lifted him vertically and sat him on a nearby stool. "I'm straight," he said with a laugh.

"Yeah, so's Alice in Wonderland," the kid replied.

"But I am, mate. I'm lookin' after me mate here to make sure he doesn't go off with any undesirables."

Twinky looked at Aaron with skepticism. "If you're straight," he said, "I'm the belle of the ball."

"But you are anyway," my big mate insisted. "You don't have to prove it."

I thought to myself, *flattery will get you anywhere but also get you into big trouble, Aaron baby.*

"What about a kiss, then?" said Frankie—his name, as I found out later.

"There's only one bloke I'd kiss, and that's my mate here," said Aaron in his casual and coolest possible manner. "And I am straight."

"You're the hottest man here," said Frankie, "but you're full of shit."

Even with the thumping of the music we were in a quieter corner of the main bar, and some of Frankie's friends gathered around. They were younger than us: some of them were really nice to talk to and interested in our story.

"Bush Camp," said one of the ruder belles. "You two are an item, aren't you? One pretends he's not—" He waved his hands toward Aaron. "—so, you can make up a threesome."

I felt Aaron's arms slip around me from behind again in protector mode, his chin resting on my shoulder.

"He says the only guy he'd kiss is his mate here," said Frankie with a smirk.

"Have a drink," said a voice. "What would you like?"

We turned toward the guy, somewhat older and well-dressed, who smiled at Aaron. "I'm Greg," he said and repeated, "what would you like?"

"I'll have one of those Hawaiian Hammers," said Aaron, pointing to the menu on the bar.

"And you, my friend?" he said, pointing to me.

"Thanks," I said, "but I'm happy with my beer."

I thought for a moment Greg, our benefactor, wanted something in return for his generosity, but it wasn't the case. He appeared to be a mature and genuine bloke, who simply wanted to engage us in normal conversation, something that couldn't happen with our twinkie friends, who had a more physical agenda. He'd also come from the bush some years ago, and the concept of two friends having a night out together, one gay and the other straight, was familiar to him. Greg's mate later married a girl from their hometown, but after all these years they were still in regular contact.

"He comes to Melbourne for a weekend with me." He smiled. "I don't think the little missus approves. She can't get her head around the concept."

Aaron's eyes sparkled, and I wondered if Greg's mate was as protective of him as Aaron was of me!

The beat quickened, the decibels increased, and we found ourselves dragged onto the dance floor again. It was hot, so I whipped off my T-shirt and stuffed it into my belt, and Aaron copied me. We were suddenly surrounded by a mob, everyone bopping along, and those closest with their hands where they shouldn't be. A magnificent dark-skinned African boy took a shine to me, making a "choo-choo" sound as we danced together with him behind me, no doubt imitating a train. Aaron's face darkened again momentarily, but then it was drinks time again as he threw down two Hawaiian Hammers in quick succession. I had a nice glass of red wine and made sure our friend Greg had a fresh drink.

Then it was showtime. I was confused because there was the sound of blaring wind instruments that sounded suspiciously like the "Trumpet Voluntary." A huge figure marched onto the stage with hair that seemed to reach to the ceiling. It was Hyper Ventilating, dressed more lavishly than at the restaurant, but there was no doubt it was her.

"Daaarlings," she roared, "we have some country visitors tonight, Nick and Aaron. Identify yourselves, daarlings!"

We walked toward her, waving our hands as several hundred queens glared nastily.

"Welcome, darlings," she roared. "You have beautiful old-fashioned manners, which many of your city cousins couldn't spell, let alone fucking practice! So, in your honor, we're having an ABBA night. Enjoy!" There was an answering groan from the city queens, which was drowned out by the first track. "Gimme! Gimme! Gimme! (A Man After Midnight)" rang out as the lights came up. Hyper was Agnetha, I thought. Another, shorter belle was Anni-Frid. Then the two boys, Benny and Bjorn. Aaron and I made eye contact. No one could hear anything anyway, but there was something amazing about two drag queens dressing up as men! They sent themselves up but performed their hearts out—none of which was mimed! Close your eyes and it could have been ABBA!

AFTER THE show, the sweaty, tempting twinkies gathered around us, trying to grope everything both above and below the belt.

"Don't you even kiss?" shouted Frankie at Aaron.

"I told ya, there's only one bloke I kiss," Aaron said, and the next moment, soft lips and a naughty tongue worked their magic on me. I panicked because my instant reaction was below the belt as an uninhibited Aaron relentlessly plundered my lips and mouth.

Our friend Greg laughed at the twinkies, who stood around with their mouths open like a group of village idiots. "Told ya they're an item," said Frankie, and they finally moved away.

Aaron decided he'd have another Hawaiian Hammer, and I could see it was all over for him tonight. He settled back on the barstool, and I took his arm.

"It's late, Aaron. We're going home. You don't need to get done for drunk and disorderly."

"I'm not drunk, I'm jus' happy."

"Oh, Nick," said Greg, "I'm sorry. I shouldn't have bought him all those drinks, but he seemed to be enjoying them so much. Would you like some assistance to get him home?"

We made it across the street with Aaron speaking Swahili or something similar, not a language either Greg or I were familiar with. Within sight of our lodgings, Aaron grabbed hold of a fire hydrant and tried to make love to it. Giving up, he slid down its length and emptied the content of his stomach into the gutter beside it.

Greg went white. "My constitution can't handle that," he said. "Can you manage now, Nick?"

I laughed as Greg backed away with his hand over his mouth. I'd made a great new friend, we had each other's phone numbers, and I was sure our paths would cross again soon. I kissed him on the cheek and thanked him as he fled.

CHAPTER 11
CHANGING TIMES

I DROVE into the Murphy's yard. Aaron kissed me goodbye on the cheek as he grabbed his bag. "Great weekend, Nicky boy." He smiled and was gone.

I walked into the kitchen at home, Mum greeted me with a hug and a kiss, and Alex greeted me with "Hello, bitch, get your dick wet?"

"Alexandra," said Mum, pretending to be horrified while I stood there.

"Well?" asked Alex.

"That's for me to know and for you to wonder at, Ms. Williams."

"Okay," she said, cocking her head toward Mum, "tell me later." She ran out the door to finish her chores.

"She won't let up until you give her all the gory details, dear."

"Well, there are none, really. Aaron and I had a great time, met some nice people, and danced the night away. Mind you, I'd rather have my head than his today. He's not a well boy."

"That's the Irish for you, dear." Mum smiled. I thought she looked a little sad when she said "Irish," and my heart nearly stopped.

"Mum. Something's worrying you. What is it?" I asked.

"Oh, it's nothing, dear. I'm just running some numbers around in my head. A typical accountant, that's me."

"Mum, you're not typical anything, and you're not very good at keeping secrets from me either." She smiled her lovely smile, and I could easily imagine how our father fell for her as a young Indian student—beautiful dark, flawless skin and a dazzling white smile, bright as ever today.

"Deepika wants to sell the hostel," she said, "and has given me first option."

"How much?"

"Two million dollars."

"It has some farmland, doesn't it?"

"Yes, about a hundred acres."

Alex and I exchanged one of our "looks." Deepika was an old acquaintance of Mum's from Mumbai. She had a somewhat negative view on the younger generation, but like most Indian people, she had worked long and hard. She was much older than Mum, explaining some of her misgivings about people in our age group. We agreed she wasn't all that smart, also.

"What do we have on the mortgage here?" I asked Mum.

"About three hundred thousand, dear."

"We don't have the people to run two businesses, and you don't have much superannuation. Mum, it's a no-brainer. We should sell this place. We don't need to generate more debt. This would give us an opportunity to rid ourselves of debt completely."

"But dear, we won't have any income from the land initially, just a share in the hostel split between you, Alexandra, and myself."

"So, you've thought it through already," I said poking fun at her. She looked crestfallen, and I went over and cuddled her. "Mum, you deserve to have a life. It's been so lonely for you since Dad left us. Alex and I will adapt, but you have your friends in Geelong, all the theatrical attractions, and a new career."

"But what about the Murphys," she said, her bottom lip trembling, "particularly Aaron."

It was my turn to be sad. I thought about how the two families had integrated and how close Aaron and I had become over the years. My favorite place was Carrick, the Murphy's property, down at the back paddock. There were a few gum trees there and a lonely willow, hanging over a little swimming hole in the same creek that continued on under a bridge and through our place. On an old tire hanging on the willow, we'd swing out over the water and let go, dumping ourselves into the cool water. Later, when rounding up sheep or cattle, we'd stop there and let them have a drink while we gasbagged. On a hot day, the dogs would barrel into the hole to cool down, lying with their stomachs submerged for as long as we'd let them. I felt my eyes mist over as I became sentimental, but there was no point. Aaron would go on, marry a nice girl, have a tribe of kids, and move his parents into town, probably in a nice unit somewhere.

"Nick," Mum said, "it's not an easy decision, is it, dear? I'm quite happy to forget about it if it becomes too much of a wrench to sell and move on."

"Mum, the hostel is on this side of town isn't it, near the university?"

"Yes dear, that's why its clientele are mainly students, particularly from India—all over India."

"Well, then, it's only an hour away from here, so Aaron and me can commute."

Chapter 12
THE VILLA PECULIAR

THE HOSTEL was a huge old building; clearly, its heritage was as a homestead, with extensions added over time. It had a beautiful, corrugated iron roof, its crowning glory. I pointed it out to Mum, who looked strangely at me.

"Mum," I said, "the only language you understand is financial, but the design of that roof over all the extensions is simple and well-built, unlikely to ever leak in stormy weather. That translates into cheaper maintenance as long as the gutters are cleaned regularly."

Alex looked at me, giving me support with an amused glance. We'd been taught by Mum herself to be practical and analytical in every business proposition, and this place would be our joint future if we went ahead.

"We must have a professional building inspection, Mum," I said. "We can't take any risks. This place is enormous—more to go wrong."

Deepika met us at the front entrance and ushered us inside. She told us there were twenty-five bedrooms plus a comfortable two-bedroom unit and office on one side of the building. "Where are you going to sleep, possum?" asked my dear sister. "One bedroom for Mum, one for me."

"Well, I thought this would suit Nick," Deepika said, pointing to another door next to the office. "It has its own ensuite and has a connecting door to the unit." She opened the door and ushered us in.

"Oooh," said Alex, raising one eyebrow, "a king-size bed. You'll be entertaining all the guests in here, then, pet. Vet them for Mum to ensure they're suitable."

I snapped back at her; this was fun. "Me?" I said. "There'd be nothing left after you got to them. You'd meet 'em at the front gate, and they'd be drained before I got a look in."

If Deepika was embarrassed, she didn't show it. Like our mother, she'd quickly adapted to the Australian way of life, social norms, and the confusing habit Australians had of insulting each other as a form of endearment.

We toured the rooms; at least the ones that weren't occupied. "There's no segregation by gender," she said. "I find it works better if we mix up the allocation of rooms. They tend to behave as young gentlemen and ladies and have fewer wild parties."

We worked our way back toward the office, Deepika tapping lightly on the door closest to my proposed quarters. It opened slowly, the resident speaking on a mobile phone and clearly wanting to finish the call quickly. He smiled, apologized, slipped the phone into his pocket, leaned on the door frame, and looked at me.

"This is Rashid Nadar," Deepika said, "from Chennai. He's actually an Australian citizen now. He's been around a long time. Originally trained as a virologist, now an epidemiologist studying for his doctorate and employed part-time with a pharmaceutical company."

"How do you do?" he said quite properly, and I found myself tongue-tied and in awe of the creature in front of me. Even Alex was quiet because no one could dispute his male beauty.

"How do you, umm, do?" I mumbled back, finding it hard to think, let alone speak. Below the belt, the engine room cranked up immediately, and I felt myself blushing like a big schoolgirl. Suddenly I realized my sister was quiet because she was also keen to get him between the sheets, so I sprang into action like a lovesick fool. "Have you met my mother, Sophia, and my sister, Alexandra? We're looking over the property with a view to purchase."

"Oh, I do hope you're successful," he said with a smirk on his face, flirting shamelessly. "Deepika has been wonderful, and you look like equally wonderful replacements." He had a flawless deep mocha complexion; not so dark it made his features hard to define. Quite the opposite. His eyes were light brown, perfectly framed by dark eyebrows. He smiled and his teeth flashed white, highlighting perfect, kissable lips and a dimpled chin.

"Well, I hope it won't be too long, Rashid," I replied. "We first must sell our own property, which is well in hand." Mum and Alex scowled at me; little did they know there was a deal in the offing, which if we agreed, would put all our plans into overdrive.

"Phone number?" he muttered as Deepika moved off toward the kitchen with Mum and Alex following. We swapped numbers, checked they worked, and then he was gone, blowing me a kiss and smiling as he closed the door.

Deepika was explaining the intricacies of the commercial oven when my sister dragged me to one side, out of hearing. "You haven't lost your touch," she snarled. "I thought he was straight until you put yourself out there, wriggling your butt and rolling your eyes at him. How disgusting."

CHAPTER 13
A DEAL IS A DEAL

WE'D BEEN nothing but thorough. Deepika was startled to find two young people who not only could read and understand a balance sheet, but who peppered her with questions on maintenance, housekeeping, credit policy, debt collection, utility costs, etcetera. Mum sat there with a smirk on her face as we dissected Deepika's business in front of her. We found the one hundred acres ran no stock at all and currently were a liability, costing money to slash the grass in summer to prevent fires. I found the fences needed repair, and more internal fencing was required to subdivide the acreage.

There was a neighboring homestead just over the boundary line; Deepika introduced us to Max and Val, a senior-aged couple who'd farmed in the area for most of their lives. Interestingly, they still had around six hundred acres behind the house on which they ran beef cattle, but they were about to destock because they didn't need the worry or the work and were planning to retire. I asked Max to delay a few weeks, and he agreed because the deal I'd been offered would allow us to buy his stock at a fair price if we needed them.

WE HEADED for home; I knew my mother and sister couldn't wait to pry the facts out of me. We weren't through Deepika's gate when Alex screeched at me. "Come on, bitch," she said, "what's the fucken deal you've been on about?" Mum said nothing but simply raised her eyebrows in my direction.

"Well, girls, Allan Finch rang me yesterday with a proposition. Southwest Canola want to buy Brookside. No agents—they want to deal with us through our solicitors and their solicitors, so we pay legal fees without real estate agent's fees. They've offered $8,000 per hectare where the median price down there at the moment is $7,400."

Mum furrowed her brow, deep in thought while Alex remarked from the back seat that we'd never get to enjoy it unless I kept my eyes on the road. "So, Brookside was 1,500 acres when Dad and I bought it. What's that in hectares?"

"Six hundred and seven," I replied.

"Goodness," Mum said, "that's $4,856,000. Are you sure you got the numbers right, dear, and why would they offer so much?"

"To guarantee a supply of product to the factory. They've invested a fortune to set the factory up, but as you well know, ours is a conservative area, and getting farmers to change to cropping around here, even partially, was harder than they thought."

"But why us specifically?" Mum asked.

"Because Brookside is flat, has good soil, and is close to the factory. And the yield of our trial crop was beyond their expectation. The only other farm between us and the factory is Selkirk—the Blackwood family. Smaller place than ours, and I think they've already sold. Same price per hectare, I've been told."

"Jesus" came from the back seat, "we're loaded."

Mum was trying to stay calm and keep Alex from a total meltdown as I pulled up at the garden gate. "Hop out," I said, "I'll put the car away." When I returned, Mum had opened an official-looking package which I guessed had been delivered earlier today as Southwest Canola had indicated.

"It's all there, Nick, exactly as you said. Well, I guess we're going into the student-accommodation business. I'd better ring Deepika."

CHAPTER 14
THE CLEARING SALE

PACKING UP a home of many years plus a working farm in a sixty-day period is not easy. It all had to happen quickly because Southwest Canola needed to sow the next crop; there simply wasn't time to stop and think. But I did think, every night as I fell into bed exhausted. I was leaving a town and surrounding district that had been my whole life so far. I'd been born in the little hospital, educated at local schools, and I had my friends—particularly Aaron and his parents. Yes, I'd only be an hour away timewise, but I knew over time we'd all lose touch.

Aaron didn't falter; he stood alongside me almost every day as I worked to first set up the clearing sale, then pack up what was left. I decided to keep the one tractor that would fulfill a multitude of tasks at the new property—my old Massey Ferguson FWA. The Murphy family had space in their barn so the tractor and other implements I wanted were stored there. Plus, a container of household items Mum couldn't bear to part with.

The Saturday of the sale arrived, and Rusty, Dad's kelpie, now very much my dog and personal shadow, was strangely spooked. Rusty had become very much a family pet since Dad's passing. Quite socialized now, he slept in a sheltered corner of the back porch in his own little dog bed and spent as much time inside the house as outside. The paddock around the house and barn was filled with trucks, 4x4s and trailers ready for a quick bargain. It occurred to me Rusty hadn't seen so much activity since Dad's funeral, and I wondered if he connected the sale activity with the painful past. Aaron opened the gate, and Rusty flew through the air, whining and being silly because Aaron always caught him in midair—a trick he'd taught him. We both laughed, and then grew a bit morose. It would be more than people missing each other, Rusty made it clear whom he loved even more than me perhaps—Aaron.

The air was redolent with the smell of onions cooking. There were hamburgers, hot dogs, tea, and coffee from the local hospital women's auxiliary stall, their business booming. We'd split everything for sale into lots. Jim Wakefield, the auctioneer, winked at me because the response so far had been so positive, and Brookside felt like a local marketplace—everything that wasn't tied down was for sale! Alex joined us, dressed smartly and kissing us both on the cheek. My lovely sister was trying so hard to be a lady today, and the blokes responded, smiling and waving to her. She strode along with us in her nice tight slacks and a beautiful navy-blue blouse that complemented the color of her eyes.

"Well, well," she said as we rounded the corner of the barn, "there's our old mate, David Lane with his daddy. Isn't that nice." I looked at her in fear as she spoke to his father, a boozy red-faced coot who was just stepping out of his Jaguar. "Oh, Mr. Lane." She smiled. "Lovely to see you here. We need everyone's support today. Thank you for coming."

"By all accounts you and your brother haven't done much with the place. I'm happy to spend a few bob if there's bargains to be had."

My mind flashed back to that day at school when Alex was less than a lady in defending me and my reputation. Aaron looked at me with panic in his eyes, but we knew the train had already left the station.

"Well, that's an interesting observation isn't it. For your information our return on investment would far and away exceed any of your properties—we simply had an offer on this place we couldn't refuse. If in the future you have trouble making ends meet, my brother will probably be available as a consultant for a reasonable fee."

"Oh, and hello David," she continued as he crept closer to his father and a small crowd began to gather, sensing a bit of fun. "David," she snapped, as Lane junior realized all his chickens were about to fly off into the morning mist. "David, we had a little discussion when we were all at school together and you led a mob of cowards to attack my brother with homophobic abuse, remember? Well now, I have it on good authority you've been giving head down at the toilets in Waltham Park, isn't that amazing? A bit like the pot calling the kettle black arse, if you know what I mean. Now why don't you pair of losers fuck off. We don't need your sort of money today or at any time."

There was a stunned silence, then laughter and some applause as Lane's Jaguar skidded in the loose gravel near the front gate and roared away. The smile on the face of Jim Wakefield, our auctioneer, was broad.

"Good job, Alex," he called out. "Now we can relax and get on with business."

CHAPTER 15
MOVING AND MOVING ON

I ROLLED out of my sleeping bag in the position my bed had once taken in my bedroom at Brookside. My phone had woken me, not by the alarm but by him—Rashid. Every day there'd been a text or two plus phone calls, desperately seeking… me. There was no doubt an animal attraction existed on both sides, but he seemed to ignore my predicament—packing up my family's previous life and beginning a new one.

"When are you coming here?" he said in several messages. And "Why are you taking such a long time?" And wanting to know who Aaron was when he answered the phone during the auction. Aaron was too polite to comment, but the look on his face said it all—my lovely straight mate was still concerned about me, like a father watching his daughter!

We set off in convoy; me first, towing a huge, covered trailer we'd hired; Mum in her car, which was loaded to the brim (with Aaron driving), towing the farm trailer; and Alex bringing up the rear, driving the Murphy's Isuzu truck. We rolled in our new driveway at 10:30 a.m. and were met by Deepika with chai and biscuits.

"Bloody ripper place, mate," Aaron commented. "Reckon I could rent a room one night when I'm out on the town?" The main door opened as he spoke, and I could see Rashid observing us closely. He watched as Aaron's arms folded around me, his chin resting on my shoulder from behind—his familiar position—kissing me on the cheek, then hopping into the big truck with Alex beside him. She would walk around our old place, checking we'd left nothing behind, vacuum the house, then drive home in her car.

Mum and I slaved on, stopping only when Alex drove in with takeaway Thai food. The beds were made, the office set up, but the kitchen needed more work. Thankfully, Deepika was a cleanliness freak, which saved us time, and we knew we'd be fully operational in two days or less.

We were still surrounded by unpacked boxes, but I could hardly keep my eyes open. I kissed the two most important women in my life good night and stumbled into my shower. I crawled into my new bed, a little refreshed, and decided I'd catch up on emails on my iPhone. There was a tapping noise on the external door, the one opening into the hallway of the main building. I hadn't locked it, and it opened slowly. Rashid stepped inside; head held high as if he owned the place. There was no smile or cheery greeting, only a look of sheer lust as he moved silently toward my bed and me.

"I have been waiting too long for this," he said, dropping his sleep shorts and throwing off his T-shirt, offering a very rigid member at head height. I suddenly wasn't tired anymore and switched off the bedside light as he floated onto the bed with me.

He was tactile, touching me everywhere, owning me but wanting me to service him while he watched on. He was so exciting; his body was beautiful and sexy, ticking all the boxes, eleven out of ten for physical perfection. Never had I been so attracted to another human being. I thought I was tired, but my body reacted as if it had just awoken from a deep sleep. I was truly revved up. Such stimulation was a dream from internet porn, but here it was. We finished in a sheen of perspiration, talking quietly as we recovered.

"Is he your boyfriend?" Rashid asked. I frowned at him, not understanding what or who he was referring to. "The man who wrapped you in his arms and kissed you this morning when he was leaving."

The penny dropped. "Oh, that's my friend Aaron. We grew up together. He's not my boyfriend, and he's totally straight anyway."

"He seems to like you a lot" came the response, but he was ready again, and the conversation was forgotten. Finally, it all caught up with me, the nervous tension, the physical hard work, cramming too many deadlines into such a short time frame. After session number two I felt my eyes drooping. It was so comfy in my new bed, and despite attempts by Rashid to keep me awake, I slept.

So well did I sleep that I sailed right through the alarm and woke at 9:00 a.m. The bed was empty as I expected. It was clear Rashid didn't want our fledgling relationship to be public knowledge at this stage, and I understood that. India and Indian families continued to regard same-sex relationships as forbidden fruit, according to Mum's sister in Mumbai, Aunt Sarika. So even though this bloke was now an Australian citizen, I guessed he too had a way to go, accepting himself the way he is. *Nothing we can't fix with a few drinks and my mad family.*

CHAPTER 16
NEXT DOOR

THE FIRST cab off the rank was to climb over the boundary fence and visit Max and Val, our elderly neighbors. I'd bought Max's cattle; they were a mixture of breeds, but they were quiet and easy to handle because Max had walked around them every day, talking to them and handling them. I said hello to some young heifers near the back gate of Max and Val's house, running my hand along their backs. They were so quiet it was clear they enjoyed having humans around.

"Coffee," Val said, and I nodded my thanks. "Max bought me a proper machine for Mother's Day, Nick, wasn't that lovely?"

"Yeah, and I'm the one who has to work the bloody thing." Max grumped but was clearly pleased he'd given Val something she really appreciated. Val had her cappuccino while Max and I each savored a long black. It was a pleasant catch-up. I apologized for Mum, but they understood how busy she was on her first day in her new home and her new business. "I should be helping her, but Alex is like ten blokes anyway." I laughed, and Val roared with happy laughter.

"She's a character all right but very protective of you, sweetheart." I looked up as they both smiled knowingly at me.

"Yes, there shouldn't be any secrets among us, should there?" I said. "I'm proud of who I am. There's no one really special at the moment, although there could be one in the future."

I sensed a sudden sadness in the room, and Val continued. "We had a beautiful son too," she said. "So, like you, but a drunken driver took him away from us when he was only twenty-three years of age."

"I'm so s-s-sorry," I stammered. "I didn't mean to open up old wounds."

"Oh, it's part of our lives now," Max said, "and we've moved on, but we still love the company of young people like yourself. It helps us to remember what our life could have been like had Stuart lived. He had a lovely boyfriend at the time, and everything was going in the right direction. They both loved the land and worked together as a team. We were going to help them for ten years or so then take early retirement. Instead, we sold the main part of the property and moved here, which was easier to manage."

"I hesitate to ask," I said in an apologetic tone, "but did you have any other children?"

"A daughter," Max said, "Amelia."

"And she's a bitch, our own bloody daughter, and her head is so far up her arse she's struggling to breathe," Val said.

I looked at them both, each wearing a broad smile, and it was clear they didn't care who knew about their daughter, knowing she'd never change. "No point trying to tolerate people when they're like that. The only thing she's done well is help raise two nice kids with her husband, Klaus," said Val.

"And he's an arsehole too," said Max. "We have the kids every Christmas while their parents are off skiing in Switzerland. Klaus works for the International Monetary Fund, and they move in elite circles, you might say."

"The kids love it here—Jurgen and Helga. They're teenagers now, very down-to-earth young people, unlike their parents," said Val. "I get quite upset when it's time for them to go home to Washington. We're so looking forward to having some young people around us again. You and your sister are as good as a tonic."

"Yes, I agree," Max said, "but we probably won't be around here much longer. We've booked into a retirement village, but our unit isn't built as yet."

"It's a pity you have to move at all," I said. "This is such a beautiful house."

"The stairs, mate," Max said. "We're finding them harder and harder to negotiate. We're even thinking of turning the lounge into a bedroom."

"You know the government subsidizes senior people to stay at home these days," I said.

"Yes, Nick, but the stairs will make this place unlivable," Val said with emotion. "It's such a pity. I've always loved this house—this is the place where Max and I put all our sadness behind us. I wish there was a way to stay here."

"I think there is," I said, and they both looked at me as if I were mad. "A lift," I said simply, "and a few bars in the bathrooms. We've got a heap of students who would love to help out for some cash in the hand. Even Alex and I, but we come for free."

They looked at each other as if I were speaking Swahili; the proposition of altering their current home instead of downsizing simply hadn't occurred to them.

"Jesus, such an old head on young shoulders," Max said. "But there's still the farm." He sighed. "It's already a mess, and I don't have enough feed to get the cattle through winter."

"How about I lease the farm from you, and you can hang over your back fence and give me advice."

"It's too early for a drink," he said with a huge grin, "but bring your mum and Alex with you around five o'clock to celebrate and we'll murder a bottle of Scotch."

CHAPTER 17
A LIFE-CHANGING EVENT

WE SAT around the table in our new kitchen about to have one of Mum's amazing breakfasts—eggs, toast, sausages, and mushrooms with lashings of tomato sauce. Rashid as a full-time boarder paid extra for his meals, but this morning his appetite seemed to have failed him. I looked hungrily at his plate, readying myself to attack any leftovers, but paused. Something was wrong. Rashid was usually focused on the day ahead, so there was seldom room for frivolity. But this morning he was even quieter than normal. He seemed anxious, even fearful, and he had my attention instantly.

"Six weeks ago, the first case of coronavirus in Australia was diagnosed in Melbourne," he said quietly, voice sounding stern like a schoolmaster. Mum, Alex, and I stared at him not really comprehending, although there'd been sporadic news items hinting that a viral disease emanating from China was headed our way. The three of us were reasonably seasoned travelers, visiting Aunt Sarika once a year; we'd heard about SARS and similar viruses, which never seemed to be widespread enough to worry about, so we'd put this coronavirus stuff out of our heads.

"What does it mean for us, dear?" Mum asked.

"Mrs. Williams, as you know I work part-time for one of the big pharmaceutical companies. They have an international presence and unfailingly correctly predict outcomes. They are never wrong on serious matters such as this. They've asked the university to grant me a stay on my master's degree because they've already begun the groundwork to develop a vaccine." For once Alex was quiet, the three of us digesting the information as well as breakfast. "The prediction is that this will be not an epidemic but a global pandemic that could take years to eradicate, if ever."

"So, what's the difference?" snapped Alex, all business.

"An epidemic is usually localized and controllable, while a pandemic is spread over multiple sites and countries, and it is impossible to control its spread. Coronavirus is highly contagious. I believe the World Health Organization will declare it so very soon."

THE FIRST thing of any consequence I did was to ring Aaron. Because he's intelligent and a great reader and a daily follower of ABC News, I didn't have to convince him of what was coming at us. He agreed with Rashid's information and reminded me that we were in a unique situation—both of us lived in rural areas, and with a bit of a push, we could both be considered essential workers, while ordinary town dwellers were likely to be subject to isolation to prevent the virus spreading.

It happened soon enough, however. Toward the end of March our premier begged us to simply "Please stay home." The entire State of Victoria was in lockdown. The only reasons we could leave our homes were for medical treatment, work or education, shopping for essential supplies, and an hour for exercise. I felt real fear, not for my immediate safety, but for Mum, Alex, and of course Rashid. And for Max and Val, who were more vulnerable than most. And Aaron, my lovely mate and his parents, Ted and Bernice. The younger generation seemed less medically affected by Covid, as it was called, but even then, people of all ages were getting sick—really, really sick. Nursing and retirement homes were top of the list, and I demanded Max and Val forget about their retirement plans, at least for the time being. Then a few younger people began passing away, and we watched in horror on television as New York City began burying their dead in mass graves, crematoria everywhere unable to process the huge and sudden volume.

Like lots of other operators, our business disappeared overnight. Terrified students returned to their homes in Asia and South Asia because their part-time jobs in hospitality didn't exist anymore, with bans or limitations on all gatherings. Our rooms were nearly empty, and I moved Rashid in with me, turning his old space into an office so he could work from home if necessary. Effectively we were left without income in our new venture, only months after taking over. *Deepika must have been touched by the bluebird of happiness, landing on her shoulder at the right time,* I thought. *We have no idea how long this is going to last, so we'd better produce another business plan. Best guess is two years of misery ahead while trying to keep our reserves intact.*

RASHID SLIPPED into bed quite late. "What have you been doing?" I asked hopefully. "Working out a way to slow down infection and end all this shit?"

"No, I have been budgeting. I must send all my available funds to my family because they too will be locked down in due course, and they will struggle to live. I must find some savings somewhere."

Perhaps I wasn't as sympathetic as I should have been. Rashid and I had become very close; he was intelligent and a loving partner, making up for his sometimes-indifferent attitude on subjects like my family and friends and dear Max and Val, who'd become surrogate grandparents to Alex and me.

"Rashid, you already have your old room rent free. I can't ask Mum and Alex to feed you for nothing so you can prop up your rellies in Mumbai."

"I can make my own meals if I have to."

I was seething, the miserable prick! "Look, Rashid, my family will also suffer in this pandemic. Who knows, the bloody Covid could kill us all. So far as I understand, your family still has an income of their own, where we have to turn a dollar in this business to make ends meet. That's now impossible because the place is bloody near empty. There are five students left, you and four others. We're guaranteeing their income by employing them to do gardening, repairs, and maintenance—and caring for Val and Max. Out of their wages, they pay their board as per normal. You, on the other hand, pay no board at all because you're involved, every day, in life-and-death solutions to stop or slow down coronavirus. That's my personal gesture considering the important work you do. You will pay for your meals, or you can fuck off. Please yourself."

He switched on his bedside lamp, hurting my eyes. "I am so sorry, darling," he said, tears welling up in his eyes. I was dog-tired but soon was wide-awake as he apologized by making love to me in the most caring, amazing, and wonderful way. Everything he did was to please me. His needs were secondary for once, of that I was certain.

"Nothing else matters but you. You are my man, my only man." He whispered, slipping gently into me, touching me in places physical and emotional that had never been plumbed before.

CHAPTER 18
ENJOYING LOCKDOWN

MUM WAS amazing, the glue that held us all together. She cooked meals for everyone—Rashid and the other students and us. She helped run what was left of our business. I watched, amazed, as she quickly put together our case for assistance from the federal government, and within a few weeks, our business was out of the red. As Mum said, "It's now a nice shade of pink. Certainly not green, but we'll survive at this rate without touching our capital reserves."

At the end of our driveway, busy suburbia began, except it wasn't busy anymore. The lack of traffic noise was eerie, but the cleaner atmosphere was welcome. The freeway on the other side of our property was almost empty, a silent reminder of its former noisy presence.

"I have just heard from my cousin in Delhi," Rashid said, smiling for a change. "It is the first time for many years they can actually see the mountain peaks of the Himalayas, because there is almost no pollution. He is in his twenties, but he has never seen them before, so some things are good about lockdowns."

Lockdown was unique and challenging for many people; the few times we ventured out we wore masks as instructed, a high-quality grade supplied by Rashid. But as a farming family for many years, then business and farming combined, Mum, Alex, and I were able to cope better than most metropolitan people. As did Max and Val, and particularly Aaron and his parents. We were all practiced in experiencing solitude, even craving it at times when the world around us became garrulous and busy.

Rashid was different; he'd been brought up in crowded, noisy, and polluted Chennai, and even though his work here in Australia was a team effort he said he "felt depressed and utterly alone at times." I tried as best I could to interest him in things outside his work but failed miserably. He couldn't see the beauty in an agricultural diesel engine at idle, or even more so under load when working. He seemed to hate all animals—poor Rusty put his tail between his legs and ran the moment he spotted Rashid. He certainly cared for his family back in Chennai and clearly fretted for their company, talking to them on a video link several times a week. Strangely we were never invited to take part in those calls, but that was his business, even though Mum, Alex, and I felt we'd been a family substitute for him in Australia.

"Our company has recognized the work we do online from home," Rashid said one evening. "While I spend most of the week as a 'disease detective,' the coordination of all the centers engaged both in vaccine development and strategic planning of pandemic controls around the world, I do from here. It is my responsibility. They recognize this important function can only be sustained by the level of domestic support we all receive."

We smiled at him. We only had snippets of information about the important work he was engaged in. Politically, there was an Australian National Cabinet, formed comprising the state and federal leaders, that was driving the research and supply of an effective vaccine and researching the most effective ways to control the pandemic. There were many homegrown epidemiologists, but evidently none with Rashid's working knowledge of viral behavior. It sounded like he was considered a hero because of his work.

"So," Rashid continued, "they want my Australian family support person to sit next to me as acknowledgment of their service and watch while we discuss progress of our research, both internationally and here in Australia. Alexandra, would you do me the honor, please?"

I'd never seen my sister react like this before. She was clearly at a loss for words, but when she found her voice, it wasn't entirely complimentary.

"Me," she snarled. "What have I done to deserve a pat on the back? My brother, your partner"—she was spitting the words out like a machine gun—"is the person who should be sitting beside you, with perhaps Mum and I just behind. Nick has done everything for you. He practically holds you out to pee every day, because like many scientific boffins, you're useless at the basics of life. Nick loves you, you dickhead, but I suspect you've so many fucking hang-ups, you'd prefer a woman beside you when in fact it should be a man, your partner, Nicholas Williams."

If it were possible for a person with Rashid's beautiful dark skin to turn pale, this was such a time. He looked at Mum and realized our relationship had never been a secret to them, so without further discussion he lowered his head, muttering, "Yes of course, that would be nice," knowing that this time there was safety in numbers and his little secret would stay that way for a while longer. That night he was in a sulky mood, answering questions with one word.

"What's wrong with you then," I asked.

"Nothing."

"Bullshit. You're pissed off about something. Tell me."

"You and your family think our relationship should be broadcast to the world."

"Well, that's a start. You've finally admitted we're in a relationship." I knew from our visits to Aunt Sarika in Mumbai that Indian men are reluctant, generally, to display emotion, similar to many Australian men some generations in the past. I thought of people like the Murphy family, who cried and laughed with joy, pride, happiness, and sorrow in today's world. My beautiful boyfriend was a closed book to all those emotions, but I caught him this time, his bottom lip quivering as tiny rivulets of tears ran down his cheeks.

"I am so sorry, my lovely man," he said, "but my family make me this way. They are indeed very strict. They do not allow same-sex relations, and I could lose them forever, my own flesh and blood. I would never see them again."

"But Australia has rewarded your scientific knowledge, made you a citizen, and we even have marriage equality. We know many people from India who are very relaxed being who they are—several of the other students are gay."

"My sexuality would generate such shame for my family, they would be likely to seek me out and kill me. Particularly my elder brother—he is suspicious at the best of times. He questions everyone on their comings and goings. He spends more time running other people's lives than he does his own."

He put his head down and sobbed, and I comforted him the only way I knew how, undressing him and making love. Rashid had kept his true feelings hidden away ever since I'd known him, and finally he'd opened the door to his soul just a chink. I mentally cursed his bloody family. Here was an epidemiologist of world standing, working hard to save millions of people around the globe, and all his family could do was to worry where he put his dick.

CHAPTER 19
A WAITING GAME

THE AMOUNT of publicity was staggering as several different vaccines were being trialed concurrently in Australia and overseas. The nation, tired of lockdowns and the social ramifications of isolation, along with dramatically reduced business and personal income, waited impatiently for a vaccine. A vaccine that would slow the frightening death rate and give us some hope for the future. One such vaccine from Queensland failed, and spirits dropped again. Another had some side effects that although miniscule, frightened people away in droves, spooking the general public and dramatically slowing its uptake. Australia needed volume supplies of reliable product as we rocketed our way toward societal breakdown. Rashid's senior management in Australia desperately maneuvered their way around the politics, the public servants, and the determination of the national government "to get value for money." Their vaccine had been jointly researched and tested locally and overseas, and their head office was ready to go with nations around the world already lining up.

"The government has lost the plot," I said to Rashid, who nodded his head in understanding but for some reason wasn't prepared to exert pressure on them. "Why doesn't your company attack the problem from a commonsense and humanitarian viewpoint; warn them about the catastrophe that will occur if they don't stop talking about saving money and start thinking about people's lives?"

"Well, that's what they're doing," Rashid answered. "They want me to chair an online session with the nation's leading epidemiologists from each state and territory and warn the government they are ill prepared and in great danger of the country imploding, socially and economically."

But my boyfriend was struggling. From his early days in India, he'd deferred to authority. Hitting politicians over the head with facts wasn't his thing at all. And like many brilliant people, he couldn't organize a root in a brothel. He needed administrative help, and his company asked me if I'd be interested. They mentioned a salary that was off the scale, and after a discussion with Mum and Alex, I accepted. I'd been doing much of the background work and engagement anyway, so at Rashid's suggestion, they gave me a lump sum to cover my work so far. My eyes nearly fell out of my head; this would keep the hostel, Max and Val, and our handful of students going into the future, whatever that might be. I knew I had good IT skills, plus an orderly mindset inherited from Mum, but I never expected to be using those skills in this very clinical environment. An environment tinged with fear—linked with some hope and yet with an uncertain view of the future. At the same time, the imbeciles of the world decided to gather and march through Melbourne's streets, protesting lockdowns and vaccination. The television news was full of it all, violence on Melbourne's streets when they should have been isolated at home as we were. They simply didn't get it, and Rashid was ropeable.

"These people are endangering Australian society by spreading Covid. Why are they so stupid?" he asked me.

"Because they've never encountered anything like it in their lifetime, and because this part of our society has been pandered to by some politicians."

"Like the United States."

"Exactly."

WE FLEW to Canberra with a positive message for the federal government, given our product had undisputed efficacy and now with national support from each state and territory. We even had a document carrying the signatures of most Australian epidemiologists working on Covid. As had happened to our senior management, attempts to speak directly to the minister for health were delayed again and again, and we were referred to public servants muttering about "following proper procedures." We presented pricing and a guarantee of volume in a respectable time frame, explaining that other countries were already vying for supply. Time and again we were asked for "our best price," like we were dealing with used-car salespeople instead of a government department.

We met with Jeremy Layton, one of the procurement people whose sole purpose in life appeared to remain permanently suspicious of suppliers. We explained yet again that our company's product had no known side effects and that we were trying to save lives by delivering in volume, on time, and if Australia acted promptly, we could save thousands of lives.

"I'll take your comments on board," Mr. Layton smirked, "and we'll get back to you." With that he rose from his chair and ushered us out.

Weeks later we received an order for ten million doses "Which," as I said to our head office, "was enough to vaccinate a few suburbs in Melbourne and Sydney while the remainder of Australians, particularly those in nursing homes, are vulnerable in the extreme and are likely to perish in agony."

CHAPTER 20
THE WORLD GOES SIDEWAYS

I WAS "rested" by our company but on a retainer, so I'd be available to help when needed. Finally, I was free to catch up with my work at home—our two properties, including Max and Val's place. Alex had done brilliantly in my absence, but she was tired. Businesses were beginning to open again, so Rashid and I took Mum and Alex to a little Thai restaurant nearby to thank them for supporting us. It was beautiful food, the enticing smells reminding me of Southeast Asia instantly.

I breathed in the atmosphere; this was the first time we'd eaten out for nearly two years, and it felt strangely risqué, as if we shouldn't be there. We were masked up arriving and leaving, but after all the lockdowns, I realized we were a bit spooked by the experience. None of us had contracted Covid, in comparison to almost everyone around us. Ourselves, our students, Max and Val, and the Murphy family had all escaped infection, which was seemingly miraculous.

"Or because we used common sense," said Rashid, medical advisor of our little group. "We continue to use masks, sterilize hands wherever we go, we don't attend social functions with many people, and we think about everything we do. We also are vaccinated four times. This is good."

He turned and looked at me, and my heart melted. "Nick and I are grateful you look after us so well. Tonight, I am paying."

"Christ, did the tiger snakes jump out of your wallet, Ratshit?" Alex roared. She was rude, crude, but she was my sister. Mum and I tried to keep a straight face, but it wasn't possible. We held our sides while poor Rashid worried about the mispronunciation of his name and the snakes in his wallet, so we made up some bullshit story to keep him happy. But the importance of his gesture wasn't lost on me. I was making progress with our relationship, and so was he. Tonight, he was almost a picture of domestic contentment instead of the mad, highly strung scientist he had been when we first met. At home we excused ourselves, going straight to our room. I knew I'd remember this night; it was the first time he'd allowed me to be in charge, and I knew I didn't disappoint. After hours of foreplay in which we both tried and did everything to each other, he gave himself to me.

"Make me your man," he said, and we climaxed together, two human creatures, lovingly folded into each other.

THE MORNING light slipped between the venetians, and I cursed mentally; Rashid was still sleeping but he always woke about now to get on with his day. He would fly around, showering and dressing in the mornings as if his life depended on it. He took the responsibilities of his work very seriously. Every life lost in Australia caused through the pandemic was one life too many. Most weekends he went into the laboratory or worked in his home office. I felt rather than saw his eyes open next to me.

"Hello, my manly man," he whispered. "You are amazing—you always know what I need."

"Morning," I answered. Yes, more had changed than our lovemaking positions. He now, almost shyly, had given me authority in our partnership, leadership in our domestic life. I decided to try my hunch out. "You're staying in bed this morning. Go to the toilet, clean yourself up, and come back to bed." I pointed to my very happy-looking member, and a pearly white smile flashed across his dark face, as he scampered into the ensuite. I did my ablutions also, and back in the bedroom, he was on his back, legs up, laughing, waiting for me. We kissed until our lips were nearly raw, and I gently entered him again as he moaned with pleasure.

"Oh, my lovely man," he said, "I so love you."

"And I love you too," I replied, running over his prostate, sending him crazy before we both erupted again.

REGARDLESS OF my changed personal circumstances in our partnership, it was obvious Rashid was useless without me mothering him in his business life, which annoyed him. Even his diary, which I insisted he update daily, was neglected. There was a pissing storm when I had to track back around ten working days to have a true and representative record of the office activities.

"What does this mean," he asked, pointing at RBB—the first entry of a working day.

"Root Before Breakfast," I answered with a smirk. "Remember?"

He went berserk. "I tell you; you must not say anything about us. I could be dismissed by my company." I loved stirring him up; if nothing else I was determined to educate him to appreciate our Australian sense of humor, although my efforts mostly seemed to fall on unfertile ground.

"I wouldn't say anything to jeopardize your career, you numbskull," I said. "It could mean Regulations Bugger Business or something similar." He stared at me, sulking again because he didn't understand.

CHAPTER 21
A NEW CHAPTER

RASHID, OVER the nearly three years of the pandemic in Australia, had been forced to moderate his attitude toward isolation through lockdowns, because it was clearly not a long-term solution to the spread of coronavirus and its many variations. By early 2022 I was working two days a week as Rashid's assistant, cleaning up the loose ends and messes he made in the other five days.

The country was back at work, but there were changes everywhere. Many industries, such as hospitality and aged care, were short-staffed because the pandemic had closed the borders to immigration. Like our own international students requiring accommodation, the part-time jobs they'd held were vacant, and many workers had moved upmarket to better paid work with shorter hours. I had a call from Paul Damon, the Australian CEO of our company.

"Nick, how are you holding up, mate?" he asked. I thought as an import from the United States he'd mastered our lingo very well. He was also a realist, having to manage gigantic egos, which were commonplace with high-flying scientists.

"I'm doing well, thanks, Paul. But playing mother hen to Rashid can have its moments, as you know!"

He roared with happy laughter. Our partnership, both personal and business, had made Rashid and me not only the odd couple of our company, but certainly the power couple. Rashid's sheer intellect, with one foot in virology and the other in epidemiology, made him quite unique, and my organizing ability had seen us working together on several projects, which had been both highly profitable and of notable humanitarian value. Pushing Australia and other countries in the region to step up to their social responsibilities, protecting their citizens from Covid, was a steep learning curve for me. International business was demanding, but never in my wildest dreams did I expect to be working for any corporate entity, let alone a company as socially responsible as ours. They refused funding from the US government and other countries as well in the vaccine development phase so they could remain totally independent and fair once the products were verified and available for distribution.

"Mate," Paul said, his American twang sliding around the Australian vernacular, "I think you and I should get together as soon as possible, please."

"Where and when?" I asked.

"Well, it's just you and me, and we don't need your boyfriend to react badly because he isn't included."

"I'll handle Rashid," I said. "I promise his ego won't be in danger, although I must say I'm intrigued. I know a little old pub in Melbourne with a private meeting room. And they do lovely Indian food downstairs. What time?"

"Let's say 10:30 a.m. Text me the address, and Nick, I'm sorry I don't want to upset my favorite couple in the company, but you can manage him better than anyone else. It goes without saying our discussions will be private. No one must know except you and me."

"Sure, and thanks. I understand, I think."

And he laughed again—what a funny bugger.

PAUL HAD forgone the obligatory suit and tie; instead, he wore smart casual clothes. I ushered him up the back steps into a comfortable room with a long felt-covered table and coffee brewing in the corner. No handshake, a thoughtful cuddle and a broad smile, as was his nature. He was in his fifties, a good head of graying sandy hair, a weather-beaten face, and his best asset—a lovely smile which drew people to him.

"Nick, you look wonderful," he said. "I'm amazed how you can make things happen, and yet you stay as cool as a cucumber, calm and well-ordered despite what your partner and our company demand of you."

"Oh, thanks, Paul, but I can't quite understand what the fuss is all about. I mean, I began working for you guys because I knew my partner was struggling, and it just turned out we are a very good working combination. I mean, I don't even have a degree. I'm still a farmer and diesel mechanic at heart, and suddenly I'm swinging along with the corporate high-flyers like you."

"Is that why you've declined to go on staff with us and stay casual?"

"Yes. I believe I should focus on my strengths and what I really love doing."

"But your dad passed away, didn't he, and you're in partnership with your mother and sister in the student hostel. That's how you and Rashid met."

"That's correct, but we still have a hundred acres of land there, and I lease the block next door from the elderly owners. It's marking time now. Alexandra, my sister, is doing the basics, but I'd like to get back to it eventually."

"What if we took you on staff for two years with the understanding you could have paid leave at any time, mutually agreeable to both you and us, a salary of three hundred and fifty thousand dollars per annum, plus expenses, plus free travel—road, sea, and air—and superannuation contributions to suit?"

"What about Rashid?"

"He's paid more, of course, because of his achievements and his potential, but not much more. Enough to satisfy his ego if he finds out what you're paid."

We both laughed; we could imagine Rashid spitting the dummy if he did find out.

"But the fact is, Nick, he's useless without you around. He has so much potential I consider your package a great investment."

"Two years at my age will seem like forever," I said, thinking to myself, "but at least Rashid will be there. I take it there's a specific program you need us to take on."

"There is," he said with a smile. "In India."

CHAPTER 22
THE TASK AHEAD

I WENT home, aware for the first time in my life I had to keep my own counsel until Paul Damon summoned both Rashid and me to make a formal offer. I walked into the office, and coincidentally, Rashid was talking to his mother in Chennai via a video link. She seemed very formal. Her hair had a gray streak reminiscent of the late Mrs. Gandhi, and I thought if she only smiled, she'd be quite attractive. It was too late to excuse myself and leave them to chat privately, so Rashid introduced us.

"How do you do, madam?" I said on full gentlemanly alert.

"How do you do?" she responded. "I've heard you're Rashid's assistant."

"Oh, certainly," I replied, and Rashid looked as if he was about to shit his pants, terrified I'd press the gay-alert button. "My family owns this hostel, and our contribution to his humanitarian work is to provide this office at no charge. I was providing secretarial support for Rashid, and his company volunteered to pay me for it. Now you might say we're a good team." I kept my tone and expression amiable.

"Quite so, but your mother and your sister have also been of assistance, and our family wish to thank everyone for their help during the pandemic. It is not over yet in India. We struggle to make ends meet and to stay safe. We must always be so careful. Regardless of vaccination status, many people are dying every day."

It was obvious that Rashid wanted nothing more than to be with his family at that very moment. Out of sight I squeezed his knee, and he knew I understood his feelings. His mother waved goodbye, and the link was broken.

"I thought India had a high rate of vaccinations, even though it's probably the most populous nation in the world," I said.

"Oh yes, lovely man, but there are no antivirals available as yet. That's why the population remains in danger." *And I rest my case. Paul Damon is ahead of the action.*

MY OTHER half's eyes appeared to almost fall out of his head as Paul outlined our program in India. "As you know, Rashid, we have very large manufacturing facilities in India. While our head office is in Mumbai, there are several other plants strategically located in other states to take advantage of labor supply, distribution facilities, and whatever deals we've been able to negotiate locally in terms of incentives."

Rashid nodded, his mouth continuing to hang open as he digested the information.

"Around the world, antiviral drugs are treated as an afterthought," Paul continued, "predominantly because they're expensive and also because there has been no education campaign in most countries. As you both know, if these drugs are taken within forty-eight hours of infection, they have the potential to save lives in vulnerable patients and minimize the effects of the virus in others. We believe with volume production in the Indian plants, we could reduce the costs by as much as thirty percent. We would be prepared to pass most of our production savings on if we received volume orders."

"So what am I to do?" asked Rashid eagerly, his delight at the opportunity of spending some time with his family obviously driving his enthusiasm.

Paul smiled at him kindly and then gave me a ghostly wink. "You mad scientists are always so focused on your research you invariably miss out on what is happening among us common people. You're well known here in Australia because of your work both before and during the pandemic, and also in your home country. As a local you're more likely to be believed than most, particularly with Nick's organizational skills and his own Anglo-Indian background. Our man in New Delhi, Andrew Jones, is talking daily with the national government and will make appointments for you in all the states, which tend to do their own thing anyway. A little like Australia but with fifty times the population."

"Oh, there must be proper procedure followed. We will never gain the respect of the states unless we observe the protocols," Rashid said with a knowledgeable imperiousness.

I placed my hand on his arm, which unsettled him enough for me to hold up my other hand, rubbing my thumb and forefinger together while looking in Paul's direction.

"You're literally right on the money, Nick," Paul said, grinning away. "The person chosen to liaise with you in each state is being told up front that the system does not allow for any slings. The only inducement is that the nominee and their family receive the medication first."

"What are slings?" asked Rashid.

"Bribes," I whispered, and his mouth dropped open.

"Commissions are always paid in India." Rashid pouted.

"Not on my watch," said Paul through his teeth. "That would add another cost of doing business there. Morally and financially, that will not happen. Nick will see to that, won't you Nick?"

"Of course, Paul, as much as I can, because there will be some hints and innuendos, I'm sure. But we'll handle that."

"Good, because you're in charge of this exercise, with Rashid supplying the medical expertise and backup."

This is really going to upset him. But Paul and I predicted this, hoping his desire to make contact with his family in Chennai would outweigh the damage to his ego.

CHAPTER 23
PREPARING HEARTH AND HOME

As PREDICTED, Rashid calmed down after his virtual demotion for the special task ahead, but in my mind, I knew he'd never fully accept the new status quo. He took to glancing at me suspiciously, wondering where I'd gained the knowledge and expertise to be his boss, albeit for a short period.

Time was short; we had to leave for New Delhi in three weeks, where Andrew Jones would brief us on all the latest developments. Every day I was on the internet for at least an hour, making as many preparations as possible in advance.

I worried about home. Mum was almost self-sufficient, having her girlfriends helping out with cleaning and cooking at the hostel, and actually managed to have an occasional day away. But Alex was working day and night to keep our one hundred acres productive and work the six hundred we leased from Max and Val.

I rang our best mate and auctioneer in our old hometown, Jim Wakefield, who was always pleased to hear from us. I explained our problem—that Alex was exhausted, and we needed to employ a full-time farmhand to help her with the two properties. "You must be psychic," he said. "I've got a young bloke from Tasmania just arrived down here and living temporarily with his uncle, Tommy Edwards. You remember Tom, don't you, Nick?"

"Yes, of course. Lovely chap."

"Well, the young fella is Wayne Edwards, Tom's brother's eldest son. Didn't get on with his father very well. That's nothing new, but they clashed working together, and Clem, his dad, is very set in his ways. He only arrived a few days ago, but I've had a good talk to him, and I reckon he'd be perfect. He's even got a degree for Christ's sake."

"How do you think he'd handle Alex, though?" I asked.

There was a happy guffaw from Jim. "Mate, your sister is grouse. If they didn't get on in the first five minutes then it'd be all over, rover. Alex is a great little farmer and a hard worker. Her best feature is that you always know what's on her mind, so I actually reckon they'd make a good team."

Wayne arrived the next day. I'd taken care to warn Mum and Alex, stressing that my salary would comfortably take care of Wayne's wages, with lots to spare. A tall bloke in jeans, a baseball cap covering neat blond hair, stepped out of his ute and walked toward us. "Keep your fucken hands to yourself, bitch," my charming sister said under her breath. "I could train this one to do tricks."

"Well, I'm spoken for anyway."

"Yeah, you beat me to him. I would have turned him straight."

It was Mum who spoke first while we were arguing. "Welcome to the Villa Peculiar. I'm Sophia, and you must be Wayne."

"That's me, Mrs. Williams," he said politely, baseball cap in hand.

"Wayne, I appreciate your lovely manners, but I'm known as Sophia, Mum, or Please Help."

"Thank you, Mum."

"Good, that's settled. Come in for a cuppa."

We sat around the kitchen table; it was more like a family get-together than a job interview. What really got my attention, however, was the number of questions he asked. Wayne had come from vegetable-growing country in Northwest Tasmania but was also experienced in cattle and sheep husbandry. The further the conversation went, the more obvious it became that he was perfect for the job.

"Do you think you'll ever go back to Tassie?" I asked him, trying to gauge his longevity of employment.

"Look," he said, "my dad's a good bloke, but it's his way or the highway, so I took the highway." We all smiled at him, his honesty and sense of humor shining through. "Dad's a good farmer, but he's wary of new ideas, so he turned the relationship with his eldest son into a competition rather than working together as a team." He sniffed a little, and Alex cuddled him, which seemed to comfort him. Mum and I exchanged looks; her daughter and my sister, amazingly, seemed to be developing a crush on our new hire even before he signed up. I knew Mum would be thinking along the same lines as I was: *What will the poor bastard think if she lets fly with her normal tirade of colorful language?*

CHAPTER 24
INDIA

MANY OF the minor Indian cities and outposts I'd never visited, although through Aunt Sarika, Mum's younger sister, I'd visited Delhi, Mumbai, Kolkata, Chennai, and Hyderabad. I was amazed at the changes in New Delhi. It had been eight years since I was last there, and it was hardly recognizable. Everywhere there were new buildings, the hustle and bustle, the bling from colorful saris, all tempered by the formality of big government. Old-fashioned-looking Ambassador taxis, ghosts of the Morris Oxford of the 1950s, roared everywhere, belching diesel smoke. Rashid, ever the scientist, couldn't understand my fascination with them and my innate desire to replace the injectors in the worst of them.

We checked into a well-known hotel in Connaught Place, and the trouble began. Rashid wanted a separate room and even demanded an upgrade to a "luxury premium room." I asked the reception clerk to excuse us and led him over to a quiet corner where we were presented with welcome orange drinks.

"You forget I'm a scientist of international repute," he insisted, "and I'm entitled to a room upgrade and to be on my own."

I sighed, studied my shoes, and asked what I thought was a rational question for me. "Why do you want to sleep alone?" I said, rather hurt that my boyfriend was prepared to piss me off so readily.

"This is my native country, and as an Indian man there must be no hint of a relationship between us," he snarled. It had been a long flight, and we were both tired, but I knew I had to put my foot down, the budget we were working to was, by necessity, very tight.

"Rashid," I said pleasantly, with no hint of the anger I felt welling up inside me, "you will not be in a separate room. We will be staying in deluxe rooms, all with a second bed so your tender sensibilities aren't offended. You forget that I am responsible for this exercise. You're just the fucking window dressing. Now if that doesn't suit you, I'll have you on an aircraft back to Melbourne tomorrow morning. And by the way, I take exception to your attitude toward me as your partner. I would have expected some support from you as I've very generously given you. Now wait there while I complete the booking in. I'm tired. I need a meal and a good sleep."

Once check-in was taken care of, I opened the door to our room and stood to one side as Rashid scuttled past me. The porter arrived with our suitcases, I tipped him generously, and he left.

Rashid stood at the big window looking out across the gardens to the busy street beyond. He turned around, his eyes downcast, and spoke quietly. "I am so sorry, my lovely man, I fell back into my old ways because we are in India. Please forgive me. It is because I do not want *your* reputation to be questioned. There are so many people in this huge place called India who are struggling to get on in the world, and they would think nothing of deliberately creating a scandal out of our relationship for their own gain or reward."

He moved swiftly across the room, threw his arms around me, and quietly sobbed, something he'd never done before. My gentler instincts kicked in, and I cuddled him back. Within what seemed like merely seconds we were on the king-size bed, our clothes scattered about, passion taking over completely. A tap at the door woke us, announcing a waiter with food; I threw on a dressing gown as Rashid bolted into the bathroom and shut and locked the door. The waiter was young and strikingly attractive, his dazzling white smile a contrast to his lovely dark skin. He winked at me, asking if he could be of service after his shift ended. "You gentlemen might enjoy some *extra* hospitality after traveling such a long distance. I could turn the bed down," he added, obviously fully cognizant of our relationship.

"You are too kind." I smiled. "But I'm so tired and very, very busy. Maybe next week," I said, knowing we'd be in Northern India somewhere, as our waiter would also know. He'd just been given "the long, slow no," but his demeanor was unchanged. He bowed from the waist as I handed him a tip.

"Thank you, sir," he said. "Enjoy your food." And he closed the door behind him.

Rashid shot out of the bathroom, pointing to his clothes on the floor. "He would know what we were doing," he wailed.

"So fucking what, Rashid," I said. "You forget we have the upper hand. We didn't use his extra services, and he knows his job could be at risk if he ever said anything. For Christ's sake, eat your sandwiches and get yourself ready for dessert."

"Dessert?"

"Yes, round two of rumpy-pumpy."

CHAPTER 25
PREPARING

ALMOST NOTHING surprised me as we prepared for our travelling show around India. In particular, the science and innovation around controlling the various strains of Covid was moving almost as quickly as the disease itself. Paul Damon rang me at 5:00 a.m. in Delhi, claiming he hadn't allowed for the time difference.

"What a lot of bullshit," I said. "You're a bloody slave driver, making sure we put in sixteen-hour days."

He screeched into the phone, and while he mightn't be a gay man, he'd certainly been in training for a while, with my coaching. "How's the princess going," he whispered.

"Still asleep," I said, "with a smile on her face." This time he roared with happy laughter and Rashid stirred. "Hang on there's movement at the station." But Rashid made a funny noise and turned over. "False alarm." I chuckled. "He's dreaming about the first thing that's popped up."

There was a paroxysm of laughter from Australia. "I shouldn't ask, should I?" said Paul, "but it's so much fun, and you don't even charge for the entertainment."

"Invoice has been emailed," I said. "Now what did you really want to talk about?"

"Several companies, including ourselves have developed an inhaler which could basically do what the antivirals do without drama and without medical knowledge. In other words, they're quite foolproof in the hands of amateurs and really effective. Unfortunately, it appears the antiviral capsules are becoming less effective as the new viral strains develop."

I thought about what Paul had said and put my business hat on. "Frankly, after listening to Rashid and remembering my time here on holidays, I think the antivirals are simple and easy to explain. And as per our business plan, we have to sell enough doses to firstly break even and then to make a profit, while giving the Indian government some assurance that as many lives can be saved as possible."

"Yes," he said, "we could make history here, the second largest country in the world to fully protect its contactable citizens from Covid. But that won't happen if the antivirals become redundant."

"Then we use both," I said. "Start with the pills and follow up with the inhalers."

"We will need to cover the cities first, Paul, as planned. That will get us to our target first, obviously. But there are millions of people living in rarely visited and/or inaccessible places that will take much longer. According to Rashid's family and my mother's family, India has been more populous than China for several years, but that's an estimate because so many births in those remote places are never registered."

There was silence, for once, on the line. "You mean to say India could have had one point three billion people for some time?" Paul asked.

"More like, well over one point four, closer to one point five billion. What we have no handle on is life expectancy. Naturally it will be lower out there than in the cities and more developed parts of the country, but again the place is so vast it's anyone's guess. We can't query the government on this. It's embarrassing for them giving the appearance of being out of control. The facts are that even with this gigantic tax base, it would cost a fortune to count everyone. Don't forget, their public service is a replica of the original British model, unchanged since the early eighteen hundreds."

"Well, fuck me," said my American boss, who'd lived in Australia for just long enough. There was no mistaking what Paul Damon meant.

CHAPTER 26
ON THE ROAD

POVERTY WAS everywhere; it wouldn't be India otherwise. In my previous travels with Aunt Sarika, I'd learned a valuable lesson—sleep in affordable luxury in a clean bed with a good breakfast before venturing outside every day. Stay in a backpacker's hostel and you become part of the cycle of poverty yourself. It was still intimidating, but Rashid and I both knew what to expect. Yes, the tide of poverty can sweep over you with constant untidiness, but while many live in humpies, it doesn't mean they don't care, or think about their kids in particular. Asked to take part in something that would preserve their health, they'd go for it, but it would be a hugely stressful job for local health workers.

We had our own small chartered aircraft—a Falcon 2000 with a range of around seven thousand kilometers, meaning we could jump from city to city without constantly refueling.

Notwithstanding, it soon became obvious that we were wasting our efforts in North India. By the time we'd traversed our way from Agra to Jaipur, Ranthambore, Jodhpur, and Udaipur, even with one hundred percent commitment to the antiviral program, including the inhalers, the numbers weren't sustainable because of the small sample of population. At this rate we wouldn't break even for at least five years, and so far as the health of the Indian nation was concerned, some other terrible health calamity could be in place long before we'd completed the task.

We headed back to Delhi, and I rang Andrew Jones to set up a meeting, Rashid looking nonplussed with the energy and urgency I was generating. Andrew met us in the foyer of our hotel, a graying, middle-aged man in a light-colored business suit, looking quite dapper. Andrew's appearance belied the powerhouse within. Not only did he understand all the cultural and racial implications of Mother India, but he also understood the caste system and its ever-changing nature. India had become his home. Like myself he had an Anglo-Indian background, but he'd been drawn back by the mystery and challenges of South Asia.

"I've been speaking to Paul," he said, "and I think we should have a proper launch here in Delhi. We've done the preliminary work. As you'd expect, Nick—every hospital, surgery, many shopping centers, television commercials, and of course social media. Give us another three days and we can launch the program properly. I'll get the troops out in Mumbai immediately so you can start there the day after you finish here in Delhi."

He turned to Rashid, and it was then I learned Andrew Jones was a superb people manager. "Rashid," he said, "there's been much in the press and on social media here about how you've curtailed your career in Australia to help out your home country. You're a hero, and your achievements as an epidemiologist are recognized all over the world. About the only other attribute which would help your reputation further would be proficiency in the game of cricket."

I roared with happy laughter, but as usual, Rashid didn't get it, looking from Andrew to me and back again. "I'll explain later," I said in a whisper, and he nodded his head. Andrew simply raised one immaculate eyebrow, and we changed the subject.

Suddenly the numbers began to bounce around. The publicity that Andrew mentioned and the investment our company had made in India began to have an effect. The general public, in substantial numbers, began to preempt the launch activity by ordering their own supplies of antivirals and inhalers, which had come onstream in big numbers. Andrew Jones confirmed vaccinations had also accelerated in the wealthier and better educated suburbs of Delhi, indicating a recommitment to fighting Covid in selected parts of India. We thought it a hopeful sign in the face of worldwide negativity, with most countries now living with the virus but with health systems stretched to the limit and frightening death rates.

I WOKE early in Delhi. It was a Saturday morning, and we had two days' rest coming to us. The job in the capital was going really well, less face-to-face contact but much more media promotion. We'd done television and radio interviews every day while our team handled social media in the background, twenty-four hours a day, every day. I had a coffee machine in the room, and I switched it on, watching it do its magic, hoping the heavenly smell didn't wake Rashid, who also loved his coffee. His deep sleep persisted, and I took my Americano outside on the balcony. Something had been in the back of my mind for days, and I couldn't shake it. Something in my subconscious screamed "Cricket!" as a result of Andrew's suggestion to Rashid that he needed it as part of his repertoire. I was deep in thought, and suddenly it hit me.

Of course! To Indian people of all castes, creeds, and in all parts of the subcontinent, the game of cricket was the only thing worthwhile the British had left behind in 1947. The entire Indian population was besotted with the game; in the tiniest of villages, in back streets, and wherever there was a clear space for a few minutes, kids were bowling like Anil Kumble and batting like Sachin Tendulkar. When a test match was in progress, productivity in the nation slowed as people crowded around the nearest television. I reached for my phone and rang Andrew, excited with the best idea I'd had for a long time.

"Yes, Nick," said a sleepy Andrew. "You're worse than big boss Paul. What can possibly be so important on a Saturday morning after such a grueling week."

"Cricket," I said.

"Pardon?" he replied.

"If you were a full-time marketing man, what would you do to market your product in India?"

"Sorry old chap," Andrew said, "not awake yet."

"You would associate it with the game of cricket, because almost every member of the population we want to reach is a devotee! What's more there's a series of test matches with Australia going on right now in various parts of India."

"By Jove, old chap, I think you've hit on something," Andrew said excitedly, all hint of sleep gone from his voice. "Do you have any ideas about how we hop on the gravy train?"

"Well, with your connections to government, I would have thought we could become the major sponsor, push the current ones aside for a time, get our message out through point-of-sale material, television advertisements, which we already have, and get some famous cricketers from both sides to endorse the program—saving lives in India through antivirals and inhalers."

"What about budget for all this?" he asked.

"If this works as well as I think it might, we probably won't need any more funds. We're simply using what we have where it's most effective. I'll email Paul to let him know what we're doing, but we can go ahead anyway."

"You've got big balls, Nick. What if all this falls in a heap?"

"Then I might lose 'em."

Andrew chuckled, but I'd made my point. I'd stake everything on this, so I was serious. It never occurred to me that I actually needed formal marketing training; I somehow knew what was required to get the job done. The more I thought about India and cricket the more excited I became. I wasn't concerned about losing my goolies at all.

CHAPTER 27
MUMBAI

I HAD noticed a subtle change in Rashid's attitude. Regardless of his high profile in India, his ego seemed to be taking a back seat to some type of family business. The only person he seemed to speak with was his mother. I frequently overheard snippets of conversation. "You still miss your folks, don't you?" I said.

"Oh, very much, but we must do this job properly, so I will see them when we have the break we planned. When my boss allows me, that is."

"Oh, so what about the boss. Does he get to meet them as well?" I asked, smiling.

Rashid looked at first shocked and then thoughtful. "Well, it's too far and too expensive for you to return to Australia, but you could go to your aunt in Mumbai."

"You cheeky prick! You lived with our family in Australia."

"Yes, I know, and my father would insist you visit their home as an honored guest. In fact, under the circumstances, I don't think I could arrive without you. Demonstrating gratitude in Hindu families includes a lot of little formal speeches—words are most important and mean most. They will thank you personally with a gift and ensure your mother and sister also have gifts for the manner in which you and your family have cared for me in Australia."

"So how do you think of yourself, darling?" I said. "Do you feel Indian or Australian right now?"

"I will always be Indian, wherever I am," he said with great seriousness. "And I have my family's honor to consider as a practicing Hindu."

I thought that was a load of crap, particularly the bit about being a Hindu. Not once in the two years we'd been boyfriends had there ever been a hint of a prayer, no bent knee, nothing. So I could only assume he'd become more ritualistic since landing back on Indian soil. I was too busy to worry about him, however. We had a job to do, and my pride wouldn't allow for failure, even though the odds were stacked against us.

THERE WAS never any question which accommodation we would choose in Mumbai other than with Aunt Sarika. Younger than Mum, she'd been more like a big sister to me when I was growing up, and we remained very close. Like Alex, I could talk to her about anything, because we were best mates. And like Alex, except only behind closed doors, Auntie called a spade a "fucking shovel." She was a lawyer, well known in Mumbai, and had divorced her English husband after he was found chockablock up their housekeeper. She had two kids, both at school in England, their education paid for by her ex-husband, which allowed her to pick and choose her clients in Mumbai, usually the high-profile variety, who usually paid better.

A smartly dressed Parsi met us at the door—Aunt Sarika's "man."

"Hello, Nicholas, lovely to have you back again." He turned to Rashid. "I'm Benjamin. Welcome."

Rashid looked at him as if the clock had been turned back to pre-1947, during the British Occupation. The Parsis were inevitably wealthy people, and to find a person like Benjamin in service was almost unheard of. I knew in Rashid's mind there would be many questions later, particularly about Aunt Sarika's net worth.

"Your aunt is in court today, Nicholas. I expect her home around four thirty. Allow me to help you with your bags." Rashid nodded his head, clearly in shock, as Benjamin led us to a guest room with a huge king-size bed. "I hope you will be comfortable here, gentlemen. Please ring if there is anything I can help you with."

"Thank you, Benjamin. You're very kind, as usual. We'll see you for drinks before dinner?"

"Of course, Nicholas. Your aunt is excited to see you and to meet your partner."

I knew Rashid would go apeshit at the prospect of the upper echelon of Mumbai's professional society being aware he was part of a same-sex partnership, sleeping in the same room and the same bed as her nephew. As he began protesting in his usual vigorous manner, I began taking off his clothes. He tried to resist, but it was useless; stimulating his physical need won out as it always did. We slept, exhausted, until a tap on the door from Benjamin woke us. We showered together, as I insisted, with a little more playtime simply to remind my other half where his priorities lay. With me.

CHAPTER 28
CRICKET

"YOU'D BETTER take care of my nephew," Aunt Sarika said, smiling like a lioness stalking her prey. As I expected, there were no niceties upfront, just a very unsubtle hint of what might happen if that wasn't the case. "Nick and I have always been close, but when his father lost his life, Nick took over his family responsibilities with dedication, intelligence, and hard work. He managed to transform the lives of the family down there even through the pandemic, also taking care of you, Rashid. Then he went on to become an international businessman! By any standards he's a hero, no less. An extraordinary accomplishment for someone so young in years but utilizing the wisdom of his life experiences. But then, even my kids, living in comparative luxury, have always thought he could walk on water, which he probably could."

"Oh, come on, Auntie, I'm not Jesus Christ," I said with a laugh.

"Another drink, Rashid?" Benjamin asked, bearing a tray loaded with gin, Scotch, and mixers.

"Oh, thank you," Rashid replied as Benjamin poured a quadruple shot of Scotch into his glass.

"You see, Rashid," Aunt Sarika continued, "Nick and I have literally grown up together. I was a teenager when Nick was born. We explored India and many other places together, in the Christmas holidays every year. Nick has his late father's beautiful manners, holding open doors for the ladies, attentive to other people's needs before his own. I hope you appreciate all his amazing qualities, Rashid, as his welfare is most important to me."

Rashid looked stunned; there could be no misunderstanding of Aunt Sarika's words, or the potential hellfire of retribution should he fuck up. "Oh, madam," he said, "Nicholas is my most beautiful man. I will love him forever, and I will always make sure he is safe and well cared for. We are very close."

I nearly fell off Aunt's beautiful chaise lounge in shock. Yes, my other half was certainly put under pressure by Aunt Sarika, but he didn't hesitate to put me front and center on his list of life priorities. He'd also effectively outed himself in Mumbai, but I guessed he'd reasoned Aunt Sarika's discretion was of the same quality as the protection of her nephew.

AT AUNT Sarika's insistence, we took over the huge drawing room at the front of her house as our headquarters. The following day was a rest day for the cricketers, so we invited the Australian contingent for afternoon tea, complete with their officials, whom we'd briefed in detail the day before.

I explained the background to the players. No, they weren't required to put their hands in their pockets, simply play the best and fairest cricket they possibly could. That the combined force of my company, the Indian government, and now the Australian government were determined to wipe out Covid in India if possible.

"The reason I am speaking to you today," I said, "is to ask for your support and understanding of what we're trying to achieve. Here we have arguably the largest nation on earth, and certainly the largest democracy. Australia has virtually controlled the spread of Covid in pandemic proportions, but here, because of the huge population, Mother India is struggling. We've tried all methods to publicize the antivirals and the inhalers and drag in the many millions who've already been vaccinated."

I looked around the room and caught a glimmer of a smile from the team captain, which urged me on. "Some of you may consider the Indian team your mortal enemies, but they're not. They are another team you compete against in the wonderful game of cricket. Imagine if cricket were as important to the local population in Australia as it is in India. You'd all be driving around in Rollers." I looked at the captain, who blushed. "Drive a Benz?" I asked.

"No, a Jag." The room roared with laughter, the cups of tea and coffee were forgotten as they began to enjoy themselves.

"The plan is to reward all those who've come forward for this medication with a replica of the 'baggy green.' It's a very basic replica, one size fits all, no lining, and at the rear of the hat are the words Stop Covid Forever."

"What about the other mob?" asked one of the players.

"The same," I replied. "The Indian players will have their caps replicated in the same way, the same message on the back."

I recognized the tour manager, a pleasant middle-aged man with a face that mirrored a full and vigorous life, who raised his hand and spoke up. "What do you think, Nick? In what ratio will the caps be called up, India versus Australia?"

"I reckon 70/30 in favor of Australia," I said, clearly shocking some of the player group. "I reckon the Indian public are more likely to forgive the misdemeanors of a few years ago than the Australian public did. They love Australian cricketers. I can take you to any village in the back blocks, and I guarantee kids can recite all your names in a flash. We also must remember Australia is accepting more Indian immigrants than ever. Rashid is an example—he's been an Australian citizen for nearly three years now. So, while we're all brothers and sisters in this lovely place, Australia is very much a beacon of hope."

CHAPTER 29
AN AMAZING THING

THE PROMOTIONAL campaign was due to go to air in three days: television, social media, and print media. Obliging players from both India and Australia volunteered their time, speaking to the camera and demonstrating the caps as a reward for participating in our program. They removed their caps in the last frame of the commercial showing the Stop Covid Forever message at the back.

I was shitting myself, along with Andrew, and even Rashid. We all understood we'd committed all our budget and more, with the Australian government kicking in a substantial extra amount. So, if we fucked up, the criticism would come from many sources. Paul, our boss, was nonplussed, but he backed my judgment and assured me it was worth the risk. Utilizing a huge manufacturing complex in Kolkata, we'd ordered a conservative number of caps in the ratio I'd predicted. If it didn't work, then we could recoup the cost of the caps by selling them, I thought.

I knew nothing about advertising except having a gut feeling when I knew I was being handled. Like the agency executive who suggested he could coordinate press, television, and social media to run at the same time for a small "personal" fee.

"But that's already been arranged by the media agency," I said. "I approved that yesterday."

"Oh, but they never do run together. I can provide assurance that it will happen."

"Well, I'll be watching, and if it doesn't happen, I'll be straight back in touch with you."

He smiled at me like the slimy creature he was and left the room. I found his boss's number and complained about the quality of some of his staff, one in particular.

"Quality?" he asked. "What do you mean?"

"Your man didn't have the gravitas to understand that I knew he was asking for a sling."

"A sling?"

"Commission," I said. "Don't let that prick anywhere near me again, and you'd better warn the other agencies involved I'll fucking sack them if I find evidence of slings, get it?"

"I understand. But is there anything else I can assist you with, sir?"

"As the managing agency, I suggest you go through all your relationships with the other agencies and make sure we're getting value for money. I don't want to see anything more than the prices quoted or I won't fucking pay you."

"Jove, Nick old chap, I'm glad I'm on your side," said Andrew, overhearing the conversation. "This gets more interesting by the minute."

WITH MUCH screaming and kicking from the agencies, I pulled a significant number of television commercials after a few days, because the news channels and social media had done it for us. All over India the Stop Covid Forever program was generating lines of punters, eager for their Covid medication and their cricket caps. Men, women, and children lined up for hours at a time, and in some parts of the subcontinent, they slept outside, waiting for days. The factory in Kolkata was working day and night, backed up by a new one in Ahmedabad City in Gujarat.

The very next day, Paul Damon rang, jubilant. "We're actually in profit," he yelled to the three of us. "Congratulations! I think the rest of the program can look after itself. What do you think?"

"No, Paul," said Rashid, as Andrew and I looked at him gobsmacked. Rashid had never taken ownership of any part of the program. He deferred to Andrew and me in all things, understanding he was a scientist, not a logistics or marketing manager. But he was an Indian man first, and I let him go on. "Paul, there are all the people who have joined the program before cricket caps became an incentive. There will be a bad feeling if we don't reward those people with a cap. They all have confirmation of their medication status. It would be a simple task. I think that action, no matter how expensive, would have very positive outcomes. Also, we cannot miss the major big cities, particularly Chennai where my family lives, Kolkata, and perhaps Hyderabad. The cities and regions can get very upset if they are not included. Nick, Andrew, and I are well known, and we would need to be seen meeting with community leaders in those places—that would keep everyone happy."

"What do you think, Nick?" Paul asked.

I looked at Andrew, and he nodded his head. "We respect Rashid's point of view, but I do think the three of us need a holiday, say ten days away from the program. Then back into it. I'll be staying with Rashid's family in Chennai. And I hope Andrew can delegate daily business to his 21C in Delhi."

"No problem," said Andrew with a tired smile. "We do need to regenerate."

CHAPTER 30
CHENNAI

IT WAS only about two hours by plane from Mumbai to Chennai and Rashid's family. He was reasonably relaxed, because rather than having to explain our relationship, we were being feted as conquering heroes. No explanation was really necessary at this point in time. I was also tired, more tired than I'd ever felt, and Rashid knew. He cuddled me close, and I slept on his shoulder.

We were the only passengers, Andrew and the crew having returned to Delhi already, so we had the cabin to ourselves. I was having a lovely dream. I seemed to be flying along by myself but leaning backward on my back as we skimmed past clouds and the odd rain shower. I felt strangely turned on; my dick became hard and there was an amazing feeling there. My eyes flew open as we went through an air pocket, and I realized my beautiful boyfriend was giving me head in a most determined way. Within seconds I came, and he cleaned me up, zipped up my fly, and smiled at me.

"What about you?" I asked.

"No matter," he said. "We may have limited interaction when we get home, so I wanted to tell you how much I love you." He kissed me, and I fell asleep again, truly relaxed.

The captain's voice interrupted our rest as we began to descend into Tirupati Airport. We'd become an enigma in our own right. We now had television identities, and flying into a private airport suited us if we were to have rest and recreation without interruption from the media. We had nearly a hundred miles to cover in a car; at least it was at night, and we had our own driver. It was around 10:30 p.m. when we swung through the gates of the Nadar residence, in Velachery, and they closed noiselessly behind us.

The poor bastards. Wail and complain of hardship during the pandemic, and yet they live in a mini mansion.

I was introduced to Rashid's father first, a university lecturer. He was polite, softly spoken, and seemingly comfortable in his own skin.

"Ah," I said, "so Rashid has inherited your academia."

"Kamala also has many scholars in her family," he said, pointing to his wife.

"My side of the family has always been focused on proper principles of Hinduism," she said, openly correcting her husband. I was dead-dog tired, but the barb wasn't lost on me. "My family had some clever people, but I was taught that my role in family life is ensuring the religious activities of the family are observed."

So there it was—somehow old Kamala babes knew her son was legs up, laughing, and involved with me. Very much against Hindu teachings and, I suspected, damaging to her social status in the community.

Gone is the presumption that senior family members are treated with unparalleled love and reverence. Clearly her own husband doesn't give a shit for the old ways.

"I will sleep in my old room," Rashid said. "Which room do you have for Nick?"

His mother smiled primly. "In your absence I decided your room would be more serviceable with twin beds," she replied, "so he may use the second bed if he wishes." There was a smirk on her lips, turning swiftly and leaving the room with a swish from her sari so she didn't need to justify her actions.

What a bitch, not sure how far she could push me. But Rashid looked like he'd grown some balls at last.

We were both tired, and we showered briefly and turned in, sharing a deep kiss.

"Tomorrow," said Rashid and I smiled at him.

"Sure," I said, put my head down, and fell asleep instantly.

My body clock had remained on Australian farm time. Six o'clock came, I stretched, rolled out of bed, used the little toilet, and then, uncustomarily for me, fell back into bed. I was hardly settled when the door was flung open long enough for Rashid's mother to have a good look around and then closed as suddenly and quietly. Enraged, I pulled on enough clothes to hide the vital parts and stormed downward to find her in the kitchen. Thankfully, she was alone, so I was able to moderate my tone and volume.

"If you were a guest in my house, I would always knock on the door before entering," I whispered. "If you don't want me here, then I'm quite happy to go to a hotel. That'd look nice among your friends, wouldn't it? Famous person in the Stop Covid Forever program not welcome in his business partner's family home? Wouldn't that be ducky?"

The look of hatred in her eyes said everything, but she knew her bluff had been called. I stared back at her, knowing the relationship between Rashid and me would forever struggle with her working against us. But now wasn't the time to back off. I had the technical advantage, and I pushed on. "I want a lock on that door tonight or I walk, madam."

"That won't be necessary," she said.

"Oh yes it will, Kamala, unless you'd like me to put on a floor show for you. Maybe that's what's driving you, dear—a good look at the forbidden fruit? Wouldn't that make a nice story in the *Times of India*?"

CHAPTER 31
THE NADAR FAMILY

BY THE time I'd stormed upstairs, showered, and changed, Rashid had woken, and I suggested a happy ending. He shook his head until I noticed an envelope inside the door. I picked it up, shook it, and sure enough a key fell out onto the floor. I inserted it in the old wooden door, and the ancient mechanism clicked into place.

"How did you do that?" Rashid asked, his eyes wide.

"I talked to your mother and developed an instant understanding. Now lose those silly sleep shorts. I've got a nice present for you."

Breakfast was served on a buffet set by a pretty female domestic. Rashid's mother was nowhere to be seen, but his father was there with Rashid's brother Bjay. He was very affable, about ten years older than Rashid, comfortable looking, losing some hair in front, and had a cheeky sense of humor. We chatted for over an hour or so, Bjay seemingly nothing like Rashid's description of a suspicious elder brother questioning the lives of every family member. And certainly not the type to seek Rashid out and kill him on the grounds of his sexuality. Indeed, the relationship between the two brothers seemed cordial enough, and there was obvious pride that Rashid was now a famous figure in the troubled times of Covid, jointly responsible for the Stop Covid Forever program.

Rashid's previous backgrounding of his brother troubled me a little, because Bjay's behavior and attitude seemed quite the opposite in every way. He knew about our relationship, that was obvious, and tried to make me feel welcome, which after his mother's performance, was reassuring.

"Come over here," he whispered, pointing to the lounge space on the other side of the entrance. "We kids all get together for a meal once a month, *without the parents*," he emphasized. "We have babysitters, and we take turns to entertain. We delayed this month's get-together because you guys were coming. So now you must join us. It's Saturday night at our place."

"Oh yes," I said and turned to Rashid for confirmation. He nodded slowly, and I caught an undercurrent of unease in his reply. I supposed it was the normal brotherly competitiveness, but I'd already detected one massive fib, and I think he wasn't sure what his siblings would say about his past. Anyway, we were going along, and I felt some excitement at being welcomed by his siblings.

The media finally realized we were in town, and there was a twenty-four seven presence camped outside the Nadar residence. We were scheduled to be guests at a civic reception early the next week to officially launch the program in Chennai, and every day there were attempts to interview us. It seemed people had forgotten about the pandemic and focused on their first and only love—cricket. Everyone wanted a cap, no one seemed really concerned with medication, and I was sure the black market in cheap Chinese copies was alive and well. I checked with Andrew in Delhi, and he assured me all the suppliers in Chennai had geared up with stocks of medicine and cricket caps, eagerly awaiting a good push from Rashid and me. In the meantime, we had a few days to rest and relax, and a night with Rashid's siblings appealed to me.

"THERE IS a way out of here without being seen," Rashid's father said. "My old uncle lives next door. We have access to his house, and there is a gate from his garden opening onto an alley. There will be a car waiting for you there at six o'clock. The journalists continue to beat a symphony on the front door. No one will bother you if you leave and return that way."

"Thank you for your thoughtfulness," I remarked, "but you and your wife should come with us. Then we would have the entire family in one place."

"You are a good man, Nicholas, but it is better the children have their own party. They talk about their lives and loves—so much different to ours. The world moves on."

I looked up as Kamala walked into the room, overhearing our conversation. "I do not approve of these meetings. People will talk about our family. They drink alcohol, eat meat, and of course Ronni has chosen her own husband instead of an arranged marriage."

I couldn't help myself. "Sounds normal these days, Kamala. Quite the usual thing in Australia." The look that flashed from her dark eyes was again pure hatred, and I made a note not to push it too far. Rashid kicked my foot to remind me.

BJAY'S HOME was lovely but lacked the normal ostentation of South Asia. None of the colorful, garish, and agonizing depictions of the gods were scattered aimlessly around as in his parent's dwelling. It was quite western in fact, even a little restrained and in good taste. His wife, Meera, gave the appearance of a highly motivated modern woman, a middle school teacher, with an opinion on everything, including Stop Covid Forever, which, she said, "Was awesome for India and was helping ordinary people and allowing the economy to recover faster."

"Congratulations, you two," she said, beaming at us both. "You've brought honor to the Nadar family in a way my mother-in-law never thought possible!"

The sisters, Dheeya and Ronni, jumped up as we headed into a large living area, and I could see the family likeness in both. Dheeya was a little stout with a beautiful smile, a picture of health and vitality, and she pushed her husband, Sanjay, forward. He looked agonizingly shy, and I think he surprised everyone by embracing me.

"You are so good for our family," he said. "Welcome!"

Next Ronni and Krish, her husband, engulfed us with kisses and hugs.

"Oh," I said, are you those terrible ones who actually chose their own partner instead of an arranged marriage?"

"We all did!" crowed Bjay. "Mother thought she was being smart with Meera and me, but we were already girlfriend and boyfriend, and the same with Dheeya and Sanjay." Rashid turned ashen, and I worried if he was ill.

"I was the one who openly defied Mother," said Ronni with a smile. "She didn't speak to me until recently, but Father has always been lovely, and he talked her around again."

"Yes," said Bjay, "it took months of negotiating. I spent all my time fixing the family problems, with Father's help."

There it was. That was the gist of Rashid's claim that his brother interfered in everyone's business. Poor bloody Bjay was just trying to push the family into the twenty-first century.

Rashid sat quietly while everyone buzzed around him like a beehive. It was Bjay who addressed his presence. "Welcome to the future, little brother. You finally have a partner, a very handsome and intelligent one at that. You're a lucky little man. Let's have a toast to Nicholas and Rashid," he roared.

There were cheers and a few tears as I sat down and listened to a tale of their mother, or mother-in-law, who, they claimed, had mental health issues. Rashid smiled at the right places, but I knew he wasn't happy.

CHAPTER 33
I STILL CALL AUSTRALIA HOME

OOTY HAD been so beautiful; the cool weather reminded me of an Australian temperate-to-cold climate, and suddenly I was homesick. Christmas was only two weeks away, and with Paul's blessing, I booked my seat back to Melbourne. Rashid and I agreed we had yet to cover Kolkata and Hyderabad, so I'd have four weeks at home, then return to India to finish the program in those two cities. Rashid would stay with his family for the break, then come home to Australia with me.

I talked to Mum, Alex, and Wayne at least once a week, and to Aaron. Some months ago, Alex had blurted out that Aaron was about to become a father, the baby now due at any time. I felt conflicted with the news; I believed he deserved a more substantial, ordered future.

The mother was Ellen Hampstead, one of our schoolmates, and a clever businesswoman, selling her own brand of lingerie online, manufactured in our old town in the commercial area. According to Alex, they would share the upbringing of the child but not live together. I couldn't help but think Aaron had lost his marbles. He'd always loved kids, and I could easily imagine him as a doting father. But he needed someone in his life permanently, someone to help run his household and the farm while his parents retired somewhere close by. He'd always been so positive in the past, usually had a plan going forward, and looked after his friends—particularly me.

Strangely, I began to feel guilty, but I knew he'd understand I'd grasped the opportunities when they were presented. So, I'd set forth, unknowingly, on an international career that had paid handsomely, and with a loving partner. But I still missed Aaron every day.

RASHID AND I were driven to the airport midafternoon. I'd decided to catch the 6:25 p.m. flight on Singapore Airlines, Rashid insisting he'd "see me off properly."

"We will not see each other for another four weeks," he said as we neared the airport terminal. "I must make sure you are safely on your way."

"Well, now, that's very comforting," I said. "You want to make sure I'm out of the way so you can have all your boyfriends around."

"You are my only man," he whispered in my ear. "Do not forget that."

He sprayed a few words in Hindi at our driver and helped me with my luggage to the terminal door. He looked at me soulfully and in front of what seemed half the population of Chennai, kissed me full on the lips, even managing a quick thrust of tongue in the process! I couldn't believe my luck. Rashid, in his own country of birth, had stood up for our relationship in general and against his mother specifically. I checked in, then went to the lounge for a coffee as we texted back and forth. Finally, the flight boarded after a lengthy delay and left the lights of Chennai behind us.

Singapore was a favorite place for me. The lovely smell of mildew and mold usually heralded entry into the tropics, and Asia in particular. However, this time it was the last port going home to Melbourne. They'd held the flight for us, and about twenty of us sprinted to the departure lounge. I guessed my luggage would eventually catch up to me, but a handsome steward assured me my stuff would arrive in Melbourne at the same time that I did.

"Want to put money on it?" I said, flirting outrageously with him.

"No," he answered with a smile, "you might win."

"Well, that could be a good thing, depending on the wager," I replied.

He laughed, nearly splitting his sides, and at least I had some entertainment in the hours ahead, a hot trolly dolly all the way to Melbourne. He sat with me in business class after dinner, and when I told him I was taken, he seemed disappointed.

"Hang on," he said, "you're the bloke who's been driving India's Covid campaign—what's it called?"

"Stop Covid Forever. Yes, that's me," I whispered. "Ssshhhh."

He nodded his head, smiling. "And you have that really cool Indian research scientist as a boyfriend, right?"

"That's me."

Fuck, this is such an innocent conversation and so much fun, but Rashid wouldn't see it that way. He'd be so possessive.

CHAPTER 34
CHRISTMAS BACK HOME

I MADE my way through customs, but something nagged at my poor brain, which was pickled with jet lag. I walked on, able to pick my own path, unlike in India where the huge crowds dictated progress for incoming and outgoing passengers. Melbourne, by comparison, was beautiful, clean, and well-ordered, and I casually wondered why no one seemed to be wearing their masks as I patted my pocket to find mine. I stopped and looked around. There were only four people in sight who were masked up, including myself, and the truth finally dawned on me. Masks weren't mandatory anymore! In many respects, Australia had beaten Covid through good management, high vaccination rates, the weakening of viral strains, and a cooperative community.

However, there remained many deaths on a daily basis, usually vulnerable people such as the elderly and the infirm in all age groups, although influenza was also a major cause.

Take a good look, sunshine, I thought to myself. *This is a great result for my own country. But Australia has but 27 million population, where India is home to 1.4 billion. Rashid, Andrew, and I, in our own modest way, have been part of history in South Asia. India is now ready, once more, to assume its rightful place in the world.*

My luggage was on the carousel as promised, and Marcus the steward waved merrily from near customs. He'd insisted on giving me his number, which I accepted, but we both knew, due to schedules and in my case a life partner, meeting up again would be by sheer chance. Wayne and Alex waved from near the door at Tullamarine, and within a few seconds I was nearly smothered with hugs and kisses.

One glance was enough to know my sister had found the rest of her life. They were both blooming, particularly Alex. I looked closer and, sure enough, there was a bump under her belt.

"You're preggers," I shouted, and she immediately burst into tears. My dear, hard-working mate with colorful language was going to be a little mummy! Then we all cried with the joy of it, even Wayne, and I realized why I liked him so much. There was no hidden agenda with Wayne. What you saw was what you got, someone who could be relied on anywhere, anytime. Getting my sister pregnant was a bonus because he'd become a much-loved member of our little family in the process.

"You two getting married?" I asked as we left the airport surrounds.

"It'd be nice to be asked first," Alex snapped.

"Jesus, I thought I had," Wayne said, his grin visible in the rear vision mirror, "I know I signed a Notice of Intended Marriage. Isn't that good enough?"

"But you never asked me first," she said, still grumpy with her partner.

Wayne sighed, used to her tantrums, and pulled onto the side of the highway, put the transmission into park, and punched the handbrake button. "Alexandra Williams, will you give me your hand in marriage?"

"Yes," she said, "I will. But at least you could have turned the engine off first."

Then she grinned at him, undid her seat belt, and leaned across to kiss him on the cheek. "God, you indulge me," she said, smiling.

Wayne winked at me. "I like indulgence, now can we take Nick home?"

"Of course."

Mum was at the door, obviously happy her eldest chicken had returned to the nest, albeit temporarily. Max and Val had traveled down in their electric buggy, and even Deepika had called in to welcome me. Everyone was all smiles, patting me on the back, kissing me on the cheek, and I grinned at them all, suddenly realizing I was the cause célèbre.

"Jesus, it's only me, you drongos," I said. "I suppose the local press will arrive any moment. This could be worse than India."

"Well actually, dear, they did ask, but I persuaded them to wait a few days. They want to do a feature on you in Saturday week's edition."

"Gee thanks, Ma."

I kept going through the day somehow, trying to reeducate my poor body that had lived through so many time zones over the last year and finally collapsing into bed. Just before I turned off the bedside lamp, my phone chirped with a message, and it was Aaron.

Welcome home bitch c u Christmas Day if not b 4.

I was nearly asleep, but this was a command performance, so I texted back.

Thanks dick breath hope you're holding up okay.

Holding all right, but not up, u bring me a nice present?

Yes, a dildo to use on your girlfriends or yourself.

Ooooh, hope it's my size.
Couldn't find one big enough.
Bitch xxxxxxxxx
I sent a finger back and rolled over, dead to the world in seconds.

CHRISTMAS DAY was mild and sunny, a break from the furious heat of past years. But it had been a very cool season, and it worried me, a tangible and ominous sign of global warming. I wondered what the future held for those of us reliant on seasonal conditions for growing crops for stock feed and also human consumption. Wayne and I were in deep discussion over that very subject when all hell broke loose—the Irish had arrived.

Ted swept in and embraced me, as did Bernice, her arms full of Christmas gifts and paraphernalia. It was like I'd never been away! I realized I'd missed country life so much, particularly the characters. My eyes indeed became damp as Aaron walked in the door carrying a bassinet with the latest member of the Murphy family sound asleep, a little boy. Everyone gathered around, oohing and aahing, and somehow, I was the last in line to greet him, which I expected!

"Here," said Aaron, handing the little bundle to Wayne to hold while he kissed me on the cheek. We held each other, trying somehow to make up for the many months of absence. Finally, I dragged myself away to study Aaron's son. He was perfect in every way; all his features were even and well-formed. His thumb was stuck in his mouth as he slept, with a little dribble of drool escaping onto his chin.

"For once I have to admit you're really clever," I said. "Who couldn't love such a gorgeous creature. But what did you call him?" As soon as I asked, everyone in the room turned around to stare at me.

Aaron looked me squarely in the face, a hint of amusement around his eyes. "His name is Nicholas," he said. "Nicholas Murphy. Do you like it?"

I thought I'd never close my mouth again. "But why," I asked, confusion written all over my being.

"Well, I reckon if he turns out half as good as the bloke he's named after, then he'll be a bloody champion."

Aaron and I had another cuddle after that, and there were some damp eyes, mainly his and mine. Suddenly there was a roar from the bundle; little Nick had woken up.

Aaron turned to Bernice. "Oh, you got the nappies, Ma?" Bernice handed over the basket with the toiletries, and I took it. "Whaddya doin'?" Aaron asked. "I'll fix him."

A happy voice cut through the gathering, and it was Mum. "Let him go, Aaron," she said. "He could change his sister's nappies better and faster than I could, and he wasn't much older than she was!"

Which was true; this tiny little namesake bundle seemed to like me and allowed me to clean him up, make him smell nice again, then gave me a grin as I picked him up. I found a bottle and fed him with the assembled room watching in wonderment. It didn't seem the day could get better, but it did. David Canning walked in with his husband, Peter. David had been ill, and Peter insisted he retire. He and Ted embraced each other; they were among my father's best friends, and there was a sense of "do it now" as everyone grew older.

THE USUAL sleepy period followed lunch, so I instructed everyone else to have a nap while Mum and I cleared up the detritus.

"Beautiful, Mum," I said. "You haven't lost your touch."

"And neither have you." She smiled. "We're like two old girls together in the kitchen. We make it happen, dear." Just to hammer home her point, she added, "There is nothing you can't do, Nick. You can turn your hand to anything, even wiping baby's bums!" We laughed at each other; we'd always been close and seemed even more so as time progressed. "You heard from Rashid?" she asked.

"Briefly, last night. He wished everyone a Merry Christmas, but he seemed too wound up in his family affairs in Chennai."

"Which reminds me," Mum said, "are we going to lower the drawbridge today while everyone's here?"

"Yes, let's do it around four o'clock. Even if it doesn't involve everyone, their experience and even advice is something I value."

WE SAT around the now-empty dining table while Peter made coffee for everyone. "It's lovely to have all our mates here," I said as my sister made gagging sounds, sending me up. "Oh thanks. Isn't it too late in the day for morning sickness?"

Everyone laughed; it was situation normal in the Williams household.

"Firstly," I continued, "Wayne has recently bought into the Williams family company, which is the best news ever. He's been doing my share around here while I've been away, and he's helped Mum and Alex with the hostel. We've actually made a few dollars out of our little farm, and Max and Val's, which we lease." Everyone looked at me expectantly, sensing there was more.

"We've decided to turn most of our one hundred acres into a housing subdivision," I said. "I started the process and Mum, Alex, and Wayne and got the necessary approvals through council in record time. The roads, sewerage, and drainage have already begun."

Ted and Bernice Murphy sat with their mouths open while Aaron smiled at me as if he expected nothing less. Max and Val were in the loop, so they weren't surprised, but poor Deepika was trying desperately to catch up, her mouth open, a real risk of catching flies.

"Why sell your little farm?" asked Deepika, which irritated me because she'd done nothing with the block when she owned it.

"Deepika," I said, "it's not possible to make a worthwhile return from it, even with Max and Val's place thrown in, and we can only see the situation worsening."

"Oh," she said, "how do you mean?" She looked at Mum as if expecting she'd chastise me for being such a naughty boy, when Mum and I had masterminded the deal together.

"Global warming is having a real effect up here," I replied. "Not so much for the Murphy family because they're in the rain shadow of the Otways, but farming in this place is becoming increasingly unreliable. It's either a feast or famine. We'll leave five acres around the hostel because we'll have to extend it now the government is encouraging students to return, particularly those from India." David Canning nodded his approval because, as he said, "It was such common sense."

Ted and Bernice looked a little sad, probably because my farming days seemed at an end—Ted reckoned I was a better farmer than my dad had been, and so did Dad. He'd told me so just before the accident. Said it was a gift or something like that, and I sniffed a bit, remembering. Mum caught my line of thought, smiled and nodded, and we were good again.

A tap at the front door sounded, which was unusual, particularly so late in the day, and Christmas Day at that. Alex sprang to her feet; and I noticed David smile, his hands crossed over his broad tummy. I could hear muted voices in the hallway as she ushered in an attractive young woman in her thirties with a smart-looking attaché case.

"Come in, love," Alex said. "Everyone, this is Marcia Blackman. She's going to marry Wayne and me."

Mum and I looked at each other. "When?" asked Mum.

"Now," Alex replied, and I thought I'd never close my mouth again. Both Wayne and Alex were dressed slightly more upmarket than normal, but I hadn't thought any more about it. Everyone straightened themselves up and ran to the toilets to apply makeup, given five whole minutes to get ready.

Mum and I had a cuddle, and she was a little tearful, but both of us were delighted.

"You've been a father to your sister since Dad left us," she said, and I lost it. A hand slipped around me from behind, and I was drawn into Aaron's gentle embrace, his chin resting on my shoulder as he'd done so many times in the past—particularly at life-changing moments.

"We couldn't stop her swearing, Sophia, but Wayne has. She's almost feminine these days," Aaron said. We all laughed together, but Mum became serious for a moment.

"You guys will always be important to Alexandra." She smiled. "But Wayne loves you too. He looks to you both for guidance in so many ways. This is a match made in heaven, make no mistake."

I leaned back comfortably and got an answering squeeze from my best mate.

CHAPTER 35
KOLKATA

I WAS about to confirm my flight to Kolkata when I had an urgent email from Rashid.

Family business is nearly finished, can we postpone Kolkata for three days?

Okay I wrote back, *can't wait to c u email new flight number.*

I rang Paul, our boss, and he was understanding. "I respect his knowledge of local affairs over there. He's a smart cookie when he wants to be, your other half. He wouldn't recommend Kolkata and Hyderabad if they weren't worthwhile."

I managed to score a discounted seat and found myself in Kolkata the day before Rashid was due to arrive. Kolkata had been the headquarters of the British East India Company, and some parts of the city remained almost the same as when the Poms left in 1947. I marveled at the multistoried buildings made from house bricks, so beautifully done a micrometer could have been used to measure their exactness. I laughed at the old trams, clanking and groaning on their rails, the same system in use since the 1920s. First class was at the front, second at the rear, the only difference being that first had a fan—which usually didn't work anyway. However, since I last visited with Aunt Sarika, the beautiful municipal gardens had fallen into disrepair, and the streets seemed overburdened with people—even for India. I asked Rama, the guy from reception, where the crowds had come from, and he smiled.

"Ah, sir they are Bangladeshis," he replied. "The border here is very porous, and they move here all the time. But they work hard, dress well, and are good citizens, although we have to feed them all."

I remembered an old family home, which had been part of the tour Aunt Sarika and I had taken, and I found it easily, thanks to a taxi driver keen to boost his income for the day. The place was full of living history: antiques, paintings, precious jewelry, all reminders of the colonial history of India. There was an original Monet hanging in the stairwell, unprotected and unattended, probably never moved since it was hung there. The original owner of the house was a tea merchant, fully engaged with the captains of the clipper ships, taking his cargo of tea to Europe and the United Kingdom. Because they returned to India mostly empty, the merchant trained the captains to seek out beautiful objets d'art and buy them for him.

Dad once said I was a good farmer, but that I was also a dreamer, and this was such a time. I allowed my mind to wander. I could imagine Rashid, dressed to the nines, and myself in the huge banquet room, with our children lined up on either side of the table, servants flitting around attending to our every need. I shook my head; I was a stupid fool in love, I thought, but my whole being ached for his presence. I'd fallen hard for this bloke, and I was in much further than I originally thought possible. Only a few weeks ago, before Christmas, he'd made no pretense of his feelings, even in public—a dramatic change from the earlier times both at home in Australia and in India. I felt my excitement build. If he could be so open now in India, what would he be like when we went home to Australia?

When he came to meet me, he seemed to be *larger,* seemingly full of confidence, a far cry from the ever-so-slightly stooped, studious academic. With a huge smile, he embraced me, his white smile blazing over his dark complexion, wearing pants that were obviously a size too small. With only one bag, we were quickly in the hire car and on our way to the hotel, hardly able to keep our hands to ourselves. We ran past Rama at reception. The soul of discretion, a subtle smile on his face, he knew my business partner was arriving today, already booked in, but in the same room. It was an old-fashioned hotel, very much of an earlier time, with a big comfy bed, heaps of pillows, and netting and drapes over the windows.

Rashid's shoes were off as I closed the door, and our clothes went flying everywhere as we somehow made love among the detritus. He wanted only one thing, which I found unusual, but didn't have time to dwell on— he wanted me to fuck him! We're both very versatile, but we made love countless times that night, and he was always on the bottom.

"I just want to feel like you own me, lovely man," he said, and I thought, *Who I am to argue?*

The Kolkata and Hyderabad exercises were all ours. Andrew Jones and his team had decided to stay in Delhi, where the fulfillment task of the cricket caps was still in full swing, rewarding those who'd sourced the medications. Repeatedly, customers signed up for more antivirals and inhalers trying to milk the system for more cricket caps, such was their popularity. Our first official task was to attend a welcome morning tea at the office of the deputy mayor, who was responsible for matters of health.

But the mayor himself also attended, a pleasant fellow, sharp as a tack and wearing a huge mustache that covered much of his face.

Thank Christ Andrew Jones isn't here, I remember thinking, because he would have made a soto voce comment about the hairy appendage, bringing immediate discomfort to us visitors. I missed Andrew so much because I couldn't share that type of humor with Rashid; he simply didn't get it. The conversation suddenly turned political, suggesting the "dolts in Delhi" had left Kolkata last on the list as usual, and they had no idea how to run the program. I apologized on behalf of both the Indian and—to their surprise— the Australian governments and locking eyes with Rashid, promised we'd have reinforcements to help advise them before the day was out.

Rashid and I started the local process, lining up meetings with the health authorities. I excused myself and spoke to Andrew. Bless him, he understood immediately what was needed, arriving on the early evening flight from Delhi, together with two of the more sensible and proactive people from the health department.

With the help of advertising approved by Paul, we began slowly but were building numbers every day. We wore our own cricket caps and there were press and radio interviews. Quite suddenly, after a week of hammering the airwaves, Rashid became the hero once again. The local paper, the *Anandabazar Patrika*, showed Rashid in full batting attire, with me bowling. The place went berserk, the numbers continued to grow exponentially, but for a place with a population of fifteen million, something was wrong. A higher result per capita than anywhere in India! Even Bangalore, with a population of around thirteen million, had less than half the result per capita than Kolkata, and we had seemingly thousands ahead of us.

"We're treating Southwest Bangladesh as well, Andrew," I said, pointing to the numbers of patients without Indian identification. "The trouble is they all live in Kolkata. What do we do now?"

I spoke to my boss back in Sydney and his response was typical. "Keep going, pet, until someone in higher authority tells you to stop," he said.

"Who," I said, "God?" There was a peal of maniacal laughter from Paul. "Are you sure you're straight?" I asked him.

"I'm not sure," he said, "but you guys have all the fun."

Andrew spoke to his contacts in Delhi, and to our surprise there was immediate agreement to continue the program until all available people had received their medication.

This makes all this shit worthwhile, I thought happily. *The Indian government cares about people no matter their nationality.*

CHAPTER 36
HYDERABAD

IT WAS like we had arrived in another country. I remembered my previous visit some years ago with Aunt Sarika; even then it had been so different from other parts of India, but this time it was breathtaking. Gone was the inherent untidiness of other cities. Gangs of cleaners were working everywhere, keeping the streets and surroundings spotless and well-ordered. It reminded me of Singapore so much. On the drive from the airport, bougainvillea and other tropical plants lined the roadway, with not a scrap of paper in sight. This place was the fourth largest city of India, with a complicated and vibrant history. It was probably the most anglicized city in India—their wealthy society more closely aligned to the British.

After Partition in 1947, the ruling Nizam of Hyderabad, (a Muslim leader ruling over a majority population of Hindus) sought to set up an independent state, but India's patience wore thin, and they took Hyderabad by military force in 1948. From 1956 to 2014, Hyderabad was the capital of Andhra Pradesh state, but with the creation of Telangana from Andhra Pradesh in 2014, it was redesignated as the capital of both states.

Its notoriety didn't stop there; the history of the royal family, through the various Aga Khans down through the centuries, and examples of their amazing wealth were everywhere, in wonderful museums and architecture. With no executive power remaining, the "family," who appeared to be half the state, decided to contest the remaining estate, which seemed to tickle Rashid's fancy. As it turned out, I probably knew more about this place than he did, which seemed to amaze him!

There was none of the procrastination experienced in Kolkata. These guys were waiting for us. A highly educated and capable group who just wanted their city as clear of Covid as humanly possible, and as quickly as possible.

"Why is this so?" asked Rashid, amazed at their preparedness.

"Because this place has a highly organized film industry, including the largest film studio on the planet. The IT industry here shades Bangalore and Kolkata put together. The airport here is one of the busiest in India, with huge numbers of overseas visitors coming and going daily, so they need to be assured the place is as safe as it can be."

Andrew took over for us; it was already a done deal after the first week, as citizens lined up for the antivirals and the inhalers in a most orderly manner. The numbers were stupendous. The cricket caps as an incentive, we were told, weren't necessary, as everyone understood the importance of being a safe haven for tourists, despite the various strains of the virus becoming weaker as they developed.

"But" we were told by a film executive, "the new strains are even more infectious, so they still have the potential to severely disrupt business if we aren't prepared as well as we could possibly be."

"By Jove, old chap, this is remarkable," chortled Andrew. "Not only do the film studios want to buy all our supplies, but they want to employ all of us to meet international arrivals and ensure they're safe before entering studio property!"

Rashid's eyes gleamed. I'd noticed he seemed much more focused on financial matters since the Christmas break but then put it out of my head. When he looked interested, I told him to forget about it. We'd virtually completed our huge assignment, and it was time to go home to Australia.

"We need to get back to Chennai and your family before going home," I said, and once again, he gave me one of those looks that puzzled me. His was the most unreadable face I'd ever encountered.

CHAPTER 37
THE BEGINNING OF THE END

I RECOGNIZED the driver, a friend of the Nadar family who had whisked us away from the media a few months ago and who drove me to the airport before Christmas. He was as taciturn as ever, not the type to have around if you were planning a party. There was zero reaction; he only responded to family, and I had a vision of him standing in the corner, wordless until he was needed again. Rashid gabbled a few phrases in Hindi to him, and he set off, his eyes on the teeming traffic, disinterested in the happenings in the back seat. I pointed to the Velachery sign as we turned in a completely different direction, but Rashid smiled at me.

"Different destination, my lovely man, and a big surprise."

What the fuck is going on? I asked myself. My mind teemed with possibilities. While we hadn't discussed the move back to Australia in detail, I knew most of his stuff was there anyway. *Perhaps he's stored all his childhood memorabilia somewhere, and I have to pay for it to be shipped home to Geelong.*

Finally, I recognized a busy road quite near Bjay's house. "Ah, we're going to see Bjay and Meera," I said.

"No, but close by." He smiled, rubbing me intimately and causing my usual response, which would be difficult to hide anywhere, particularly in public.

"You'd better stop that," I said, "unless you can find somewhere a little more private."

"Oh, we will," he said. "Somewhere very private."

We turned into quite a nice street, reasonably clean, mainly free of rubbish, and with some struggling but cooling greenery that billowed out over footpaths. Our driver had clearly been here before. He knew where to go, pulling into a laneway with an impressive residence at the front. We idled down to another house at the rear of the block, which was much smaller but seemed neat and clean from outside. We alighted, me still with a stiffy, and looked around.

"Well, darling man, what do you think?" Rashid asked.

"What do I think about what?" I replied, my erection wilting away as the conversation became more serious.

"This is your new home. It is my gift to you, my beautiful man," he said expansively, waving his hand toward the smaller building like a magician.

"Well, that's very nice," I said. "An investment in Chennai. At least your family could look after the tenants for you."

"No," Rashid replied, stamping his foot in frustration. "This is where you live forever."

"But we agreed we would live in Geelong, near my family. We discussed this many times. I didn't belabor it because we were so busy, but not once did you suggest we should live in India, because I would have told you immediately No way, Jose."

"What is this, Jose?" Rashid asked, reverting back to his Indian roots, deliberately not understanding my point of view.

I was exasperated; when Rashid had a plan in place, particularly if it was his idea, he didn't take kindly to criticism. Thinking my way around his question, I said simply, but kindly, "Let's discuss this later over a few drinks."

"You do not want to see inside your home?" he said, looking insulted.

I sighed and grinned at him. This wasn't going well, but I knew it would be worse if I didn't play along with his plans, no matter how crazy they might be. "Oh, of course I want desperately to look at my new house. Thank you," I said, and he smiled again. *Christ, sometimes he's so childlike and naïve.*

He proudly produced a key, and we began our exploration. It was a nice house, no doubt, and wouldn't be out of place at home in Geelong— thirty years ago. It would have been ultramodern back then, but in its defense, it appeared solidly built, I thought as I ran my eye over door frames and cornices, checking if they were plumb and true. We finished in the nice bedroom upstairs, and I knew he wanted to christen the property with a resounding root, but I shook my head. Something wasn't quite right. I turned and made my way downstairs, opened the front door, and stared at the other, larger house in front.

"Who lives there?" I asked innocently.

"I do," he said, "some of the time."

Suddenly I was on high alert, several major questions popping up unanswered. He now wanted to settle in India instead of home in Australia. He'd bought two houses in Chennai, one for me and one for him, which made no sense at all. My stomach turned over, and I felt my heart rate quicken, aware my face was burning and that I'd lost all sense of control.

"Why are you living in one house with me in another?" I snapped.

"I live there with my wife. We got married just before Christmas. Very quick so no publicity, and she is already pregnant. I have done my duty to my family, but I will spend most of my time with you, in this house."

"What, two nights a week for a good fuck then home to wifey?"

"Oh no, at least three nights a week."

The humidity in Chennai is particularly oppressive, and the perspiration coursed down my neck as I stared at him.

"You deceitful arsehole," I breathed. "How dare you do this to me? You had this planned a long time ago, didn't you? Got me in so far, I couldn't get out. And if I was silly enough to listen to you, I'd forever be your devoted number two, stuck away in a Chennai suburb with a life as interesting as a bucket of shit."

"But lovely man, I do love you so much. I do not pretend about my love. You are my only beautiful man forever. Please, you must understand. I do all this for you!" he cried, waving at the real estate around us.

"So, if you did it for me, why didn't you discuss it with me first as I've always done with you?"

"But this is India, and I am the man of the house," he said. "I must make the decisions. You must not be concerned about any of this. I am in charge. You will have a lovely life, and I will look after you."

"You are absolutely crazy," I replied, tired of all this shit and the way my life had been manipulated without consultation. "So, you've been in cohorts with Mummy, haven't you?" I snapped at him. "You and Mummy are both fucked-up. You've pretended otherwise, but in fact you've been working toward this for a long, long time. But I'll bet the rest of your family aren't so pleased. They'll be irate. I doubt if any of them would even acknowledge you after this stupidity."

"My wife is not stupid!" he shouted.

"No, but you stuck your dick in her, you cheating bastard, when you claimed you only loved me?"

"No, that is our way here—one has the wife up front and the other friend nearby, so we are respectable and comfortable in our culture."

I felt a cold rage take over my emotions as I tore open my big overnight bag.

"What are you doing?" he asked as I began throwing his laundry out on the ground, including his shaving gear and toiletries. There was a bottle of lubricant, which I threw at him.

"Your missus might dry up," I said, "when she realizes she's married a poof, so you can grease her up to your heart's content."

I heaved the last of his stuff out and closed the bag. My mind was in turmoil. I needed to get away from this place and put the horrible images and hurt behind me. Rashid was still talking shit as I walked away toward the street. To my surprise a familiar vehicle turned into the laneway, and it was Bjay. He ran over and cuddled me. "Nick, did you tell him to go?"

"Of course."

"Good, we are all very embarrassed. Father is also terribly upset. I think our mother is destined for mental treatment, as he should be," he said, pointing at Rashid, who now stood, resolute, pouting. I looked at him for the last time. I knew he had convinced himself he was the injured party, the bond between mother, son, and the Hindu religion infallible in his eyes.

CHAPTER 38
TAIL BETWEEN THE LEGS

I FELT like a mongrel dog that someone had kicked the shit out of. My pride was hurt, and I'd been made to look like an idiot, while Rashid had manipulated me and our life together as a couple. He'd effectively ruined our future, making it untenable for me to continue in any shape or form. And our friendship was also kaput, the trust built over nearly two years evaporated in as many minutes when he revealed his ghastly secret.

I sat at the table in Bjay and Meera's kitchen, dry-eyed and furious. The remainder of the family arrived, bringing food and kids, proving there was a positive side to my troubles, and I relaxed a little. Bjay handed me a Kingfisher beer, reinforcing once again his indifference to Hindu customs and dictates.

"Enjoy, dear boy," he said. "I will have one also."

"We wanted to tell you what he'd done," said Meera, "but it was complicated because the girl's family was involved fully, and it was all too late."

"Yes," said Bjay, "we were all so embarrassed, but it was our father who suggested we shouldn't interfere, just in case you wanted to go along with the lifestyle that Rashid wanted for you."

"Number two forever," I said, without humor.

"I never doubted what your reaction would be," said Bjay quietly, "but her family are cunning and without principle, and I don't trust them. My brother is so naïve about these things. His life will be miserable. He should be in Australia, married to you. He was always Mother's boy, but they plotted and planned behind our backs. We thought you had changed him, and you did in so many ways, but sadly the leopard doesn't change his spots."

Ronni and Dheeya came over and cuddled me, both of them weepy, but they were angry at the same time. Ronni, always the outspoken one, was livid.

"Our mother is quite mad, Nick," she said, "but Rashid is devoted to her, and the secrecy over this business was because we didn't approve. I hope you understand that."

"I do, and thanks. What's her name?" I asked, more than a little curious.

"Anika," said lovely Dheeya, the cuddly one. "It means brilliance or splendor in Sanskrit, but to me she appears to be a little dumb, if you know what I mean. Her family seem very strange. They are so old-fashioned, with idiotic views about everything, like vaccination."

My mouth fell open. Rashid's mother must have been desperate in her matchmaking. Here was an unvaccinated person marrying India's preeminent expert on immunology!

Bjay smiled. "Well, you see, Nick, Rashid has a dark secret from his school days, which he clearly hasn't discussed with you. Not that anyone, even in India, would take any notice these days. He and a friend, Suraj, were caught in bed together as fourteen-year-olds when Suraj's parents arrived home unexpectedly. There was mayhem. Our father was very relaxed, as is his nature, but Mother went ballistic. A few months later Rashid was sent to Australia to live and study and eventually achieved dual citizenship, as you know. 'Just in case he didn't mend his ways,' as Mother put it. He would be hidden away in Australia, and so Mother's friends wouldn't be able to question his sexuality." He paused for a moment, taking my hands in his. "Above all, Nick, my brother has always been a pathological liar, and the remainder of our family are horrified at his behavior and his treatment of you. What upsets us all further is that we probably won't see as much of you as we would like. You were a true unifying force within our family, and we are so proud of you. Please don't forget us."

CHAPTER 39
MANY UNHAPPY RETURNS

I FOUND myself expecting two seats in the aircraft where only one was required. And two meals, with two drinks and snacks. This was supposed to be our return trip home to Australia. I cursed myself for being so stupid but continued to think plurally all the way to Singapore. I tried numbing the pain with several Scotch and sodas, but common sense eventually told me the potential hangover wasn't worth it. The flight arrived early in Singapore, and a slight delay pushed our departure time out further. I had several hours to wait. Deciding I needed some good food, I made my way to a noodle restaurant, surprising myself with my appetite, ordering and enjoying a huge bowl of seafood soup.

I wandered around, mainly window shopping, my thoughts calmer after my lovely feed. Everyone at home knew what had happened, despite asking them to keep the news quiet because it made me feel like an idiot. I needed time to sort myself and my feelings out. I tried to resign from my job, but Paul Damon was adamant. I was on sick leave until further notice, and we'd get together when I was feeling better.

I sighed to myself; I'd looked at everything of interest, but I was still a bit antsy—I decided to try to relax in the airline business-class departure lounge upstairs, even though I normally avoided their plastic westernized food and horrible coffee. It was quieter there, despite a table of Australian businessmen who were laughing at their own jokes, up themselves because of the lift in social status the lounge afforded them.

I walked toward the opposite side of the room and stopped dead in my tracks. There was a well-dressed, late-forties guy at a table, working away at a laptop with a glass of wine on the table, looking very civilized.

"Greg?" I said, and he looked up, puzzlement etched on his face, then broke into a huge smile.

"Nick," he said, "is that you?" He stood up and embraced me. "What are you doing here?"

"Returning home after an assignment in India."

"Oh of course. Little did I know one of the young blokes I met at a drag show in Prahran would end up becoming famous saving the world from Covid. And your mate Aaron, how's he going?"

"He's a father now, to a little boy."

"Married?"

"No, a strange relationship. They live apart, but little Nicky spends most of his time with his dad."

"Nicky? Named after you?"

"Yes," I said and laughed. "It appears we're as close as ever, even though we play for different teams."

"That's lovely, isn't it?" Greg said. "But nothing surprises me these days, particularly after my own experience."

"Do tell," I said, forgetting about my own miserable life for a while.

"You remember I mentioned my young mate Neville who came from our hometown? Loved to spend a weekend with me in Melbourne, but the little missus never got it."

"Oh yes," I said. "Last phone call you mentioned you had a house full. Didn't he and his kids move in with you?"

"Yes, the missus pissed off with another bloke. Not only did she leave Neville, but the two kids as well, Liam and Jessica. I could never imagine, under any circumstances, how a parent could simply walk away and leave their kids. It horrified me, so I opened my house, and I had an instant family."

"And it sounds like you opened your heart as well," I said.

Greg smiled, and I caught the hint of a blush. "Well, yes, we've become a real family, I thought I'd never find anyone who'd put up with me, but he decided to, and it feels so right."

I smiled. "Age difference?"

"Ten years."

"Happy?"

"Delighted. What about you?"

"That's another story, Greg. It's all over."

CHAPTER 40
EVERYTHING OLD IS NEW AGAIN

I WALKED with Greg to the baggage carousel; his face lit up as his family appeared at his side. Neville seemed a quiet, homespun type of bloke, while the two kids were kids—boisterous and full of life. The welcome reserved for Greg was noisy and unpretentious. They clearly loved their new family dynamic and weren't afraid to demonstrate it.

I grabbed my bag at last and straightened up when a hand curled around my belly from behind. It drew me in, then the other arm circled me, and a chin rested on my right shoulder. I breathed out. It was him, of course. Aaron. Greg was standing and watching, and he walked over to introduce Neville and their kids. Aaron remembered him instantly.

"He had to escort me home one night, mate," he said to Neville. "I was a little the worse for wear."

"As I remember, you were so pissed you could barely stay upright," said Greg, "and then you called out to 'herb' on the footpath, and I had to leave before I copied you. I'm really sorry I lost your phone number, but Nick and I've stayed in touch."

Aaron looked at him kindly and said something that sounded curious to me. "Yes, mate, I wished we'd stayed in touch as well. I needed some advice at that time. But its lovely to see you with a whole new family— that's pretty cool, isn't it?"

"Oh, thanks, mate," Greg replied. "I hope we can see more of you two now, but probably not at a drag show. The kids would want to take over."

IT WAS a quieter reception as Aaron drove into the yard. I knew Mum would be in the office, Wayne would be down in the subdivision clearing the homesites, and Alex, at five months pregnant, would probably be painting their new home.

"You want to hide away, mate?" Aaron asked. "Stay with us and I'll keep the nosy pricks away and let you settle a bit."

Nothing could have been as considerate as my best mate. I found out later he'd bullied everyone, told them all to stay home, that I needed a mate, not tea and fucking sympathy.

I did think hard about his invitation, but my immediate family would be disappointed, and I had to wind up my business affairs so I was separated from Rashid as fast as possible.

"Thanks mate, but no," I said. "I have to clear up all this mess first, throw out every bloody thing that reminds me of him, and then I'll come down for a holiday."

Quick as a flash he snapped at me with a huge grin, "What fucking holiday? I'll have you barefoot and pregnant and looking after my every wish."

"Bitch."

"You made me like it."

MUM WAS in the office and ran out to throw her arms around me, managing to weep copiously at the same time. Then we stopped, looked at each other, and laughed. It was unusual to cry in the Williams family. We only shed tears when all else had failed. Last time I could remember this happening was the day of Dad's death, when we cried away our hurt in the finality of his passing. This time Mum wept for her eldest child, whose heart had been broken in such a profound, even shocking, manner. I remained dry-eyed and angry.

Mum knew. "You have to put this behind you, darling," she said. "You must forgive him. As treacherous as his actions have been, you can't afford to join him in his lies and shocking behavior. Don't allow him to drag you down. Stay calm, allow us to look after you, and you will recover. It doesn't seem likely at the moment, but it will happen. Give it time."

Wayne had no trouble beating my very pregnant sister to the kitchen door; he left it swinging open as he bounded across the kitchen, lifted me off the floor, and cuddled me like a huge bear. He didn't say much, but then again, he didn't have to; his actions spoke louder than words. Alex waddled over to me, and I actually smirked at her.

"Don't expect me to lift you off the bloody floor," she said and then buried her head on my chest. "When I'm delivered, I'll go to Chennai and knackerate the bastard," she mumbled. "The world would be better off without a lying bastard like that. I'd enjoy using a really blunt knife, so the arsehole learns how to really suffer. And to make sure they get the message, I'll feed his balls to his silly fucken missus for breakfast. No one hurts my brother, but no one. I promise he'll regret ever putting the moves on you, Nicky babes."

Mum turned around with her usual horrified look. Wayne normally tempered Alex's outbursts, but it was clear he shared the same sentiments, and he nodded, smiling.

"This is therapeutic, Sophia. While Alex has her own way of putting things, she's right to speak her mind. Rashid was part of this family before I arrived, and you've given him everything. Much, I guess at little or no cost to himself while everyone struggled with the pandemic. I know," he continued, "that he was in no small way responsible for saving lives through his scientific work, but in human terms he's returned your love and support by ruining your beautiful son's life."

I was embarrassed at Wayne's description, but he'd certainly summed up the situation.

"Thanks, mate," I said, seeing a side of Wayne I hadn't seen before. "By the time I'm finished, you'll never know he ever lived here."

CHAPTER 41
GROUND ZERO

THE NEXT morning, the early light woke me, but I felt I'd not rested enough. My head had a dull ache as my mind focused on the last week or so. Mum had changed the linen on my bed—the last thing I needed was his characteristic scent as a legacy. But the bed and the room were empty, and I didn't like it. It spoke of failure and a life with nothing to look forward to. As I lay there, I realized that in the past, there had been always something interesting or exciting due to happen every day, which helped me spring out of bed and get on with it. Particularly after Dad lost his life, I had been motivated to make the farm pay and get on with making a living for Mum, Alex, and me.

Aaron was always nearby in those days to help, and if we ran out of work on our place, there was always something across the road at the Murphy's. And on the very day we took possession of the hostel, I met Rashid, the person who I hoped would become my life partner, and life became even more challenging. I'd changed careers temporarily, supporting Rashid, and every day became important, driven by a desire to help other humans conquer or prepare for the worst in my mother's home country, India. No day was the same. I lived on a highwire, not knowing what to expect next. Now Rashid and I were finished, and so was the job that had kept me on my toes for the last eighteen months.

There was something else, however. A flashback. Back to my early days at school. I was made to feel inferior because I was gay, not as good as the straight kids. For a while it did affect me, but I got over it, with Aaron's help. But Rashid had chosen a woman over me, and the old complex came back to haunt me. Adding to my shitty attitude.

Boredom is also a useless, unproductive state, and I finally hopped out of bed, cursing my negative mindset. I threw on some shorts and an old T-shirt and followed the only positive—the delicious smell of coffee. Mum was trying to put on a brave face for my sake, but I found it irritating.

"Sorry," I said, apologizing for my mood. I grabbed my coffee, strode out the back door, and headed for the old laundry where Rusty slept these days. I called him and finding no response, poked my head around the door. He was curled up comfortably in the fetal position in his old basket, gone to sleep forever during the night. I leaned back against the door frame and wondered if there was any other fucking thing that could possibly ruin my return home more than the loss of my old friend Rusty. He'd been Dad's dog, but mine since the accident, and usually didn't like working for anyone else but me. The exception was Aaron, whom he adored. He loved Mum and Alex, but by the time Wayne became part of our family, he was an old, retired dog, happy to stay close to the kitchen and let Wayne's loopy mixed breed, Sarah, do any rounding up or yard work. Which wasn't much anyway these days.

We found a spot that wouldn't be disturbed, away from any future development and clear of drainage issues, and Wayne used our new ditch digger to create a deep and secluded resting place. I lowered Rusty into it as Mum, Alex, and Wayne bawled their eyes out. For the three of us, it was the last visible link with Dad, and for Wayne, it was goodbye to a good mate. I rang Aaron to tell him the news, and he turned on the waterworks as well. He recovered soon enough and after hanging up sent me a pic of their kelpie bitch, Maude, and her litter. Maude had whelped that morning. It was too much of a coincidence, and whether I liked it or not, I'd have a new dog after the pups were weaned.

THE REMAINDER of the day dragged along after its inauspicious start. Wayne was all excited with the subdivision and gave me a tour. Then he wanted me to look at the lambs, which he was fattening for the next sale, but I called a halt to his enthusiasm because I felt drained. I apologized to him and went home, politely refusing a coffee from Mum. I threw myself on my bed and slept for two hours, a deep dreamless sleep of exhaustion. I woke as the light began to fade, feeling I could stay in bed forever. It was warm, comfy, and I felt safe. I dragged myself off the bed and wandered out to the kitchen.

"Tea, dear?" Mum asked, and I shook my head. "What have we got that's stronger?" I asked, searching the old cabinet from the farm and finding a bottle of Scotch. I poured myself a generous hit, offered Mum a drink, which she refused, and took a deep draft of the mellow liquid. Almost immediately I began to feel better and poured myself another as Alex walked in, covered in paint spots.

"Nearly finished," she said. "Another coat on the kitchen and pantry and we can move in." I remembered the design of the portable home we decided to buy for her and Wayne as a temporary measure so they could supervise the subdivision and begin their married life under their own roof. Alex fell in love with it, and Wayne followed. We bought the unit which arrived in several pieces on low-loader transporters, and within a few hours it was complete on the concrete slab that was waiting for it. Alex had repainted it to her own color scheme, and somewhere I knew what an undertaking that would be for a very pregnant girl but didn't say so. We'd never been that effusive with each other, even if Mum was.

"You wanna drink?" I asked.

"Well, that's a joke, Joyce," she said. "Not that shit while I'm preggers, thank you very much."

Mum didn't have to look disapproving; Alex had done it for her as I (probably rudely) let it flow over my head. Wayne walked in, and I offered him the same, but he chose a beer, which gave me an excuse to chug another two Scotches, each one stronger than the rest. Dinner was beautiful, but I couldn't eat it all, preferring to have a liqueur or two afterward. I walked around outside for a while, then decided to have a cup of tea with Mum. I did feel a bit better, but the Scotches were wearing off, and the headache returned, throbbing at my temples. I kissed her good night. The worry was still etched in her face, and I thought to myself, *Sorry love, I'm your eldest fucked-up child, and you must deal with it too, just like I have to.*

I FELL into a stupor, half-awake, half-asleep. The bed was cold and lonely, and I tossed and turned, trying to fall into my usual deep slumber. Suddenly there was a light tap, tap, and the door cracked open a few centimeters.

"You awake, bro?" asked Wayne as he slipped into the room and closed the door soundlessly. He was a sex god in a tee and sleep shorts like no one else, filling them out in all the right places. He sat on the bed, and I could see him smiling in the half dark. "Alex sent me," he explained. "I actually wanted to come earlier, but I had to wait until she suggested it, like I knew she would. She reckons all you need is a good root, and as her appetite for dick is limited these days, she thought I could help out."

I switched the bedside lamp on, feeling a mixture of amazement and shock, tinged with awe that they cared for me enough for Wayne to offer his body to "cure" me!

"Oh mate," I said, "for a start you're a straight guy, you're married to my sister, who could have second thoughts about your offer, and we could fuck up our strong family unit forever," I said quite seriously.

"Well firstly, I don' know any young bloke who's committed gay or straight these days, and if you'd been available at the time, *I could be your bloody husband now*. It's never worried me in any way, guys, or chicks. That's one of the reasons Daddy hated me even more than my brothers. Secondly, your sister is more modern than you think, and so is Sophia. We all know there is more than a relationship breakup going on in your head, something much more. My guess is that you gave him everything you had, leaving nothing more to give emotionally, and he played along, deceiving you. He not only broke your heart, but he also broke your trust."

I nodded miserably. Wayne was spot on as usual, and I loved him for it.

"Look," I said, "your proposition to get me going again is lovely and if I were in a better place, I'd take it up. But I can't offer you anything in return because I can't even get hard. It's been over a week since this happened, but my dick has been swinging around, not even a morning woody, and even a spunk like you couldn't get it up, I'm afraid."

"Well, sweetheart, I reckon you will need some professional help eventually, but you've got to realize this family needs to operate as a team, so move over."

I didn't have any option as he pulled up the doona and slipped in behind me. When he found I slept nude, his shorts and tee went flying over my head as he cuddled up to me like a big bear, cupping my most intimate parts with a big hand. He kissed me behind my ear and whispered that I should go to sleep. There was an enormous pole at my rear, partly hard and partly soft. I discovered trust in a nice way again and slipped off to sleep, feeling a little better about life in general.

CHAPTER 42
THE REALITY—MENTAL ILLNESS

I STRUGGLED for nearly two months until Mum, Alex, Wayne, and Aaron wore me down. I tried doing the normal jobs around the place, including helping with the hostel. I found myself apologizing to the new boarders as I booked them in because I knew I'd become so abrupt. I told them I'd had an accident and was still recovering. I'd help Wayne leveling blocks and cleaning up in the subdivision and found I didn't have the desire to finish the job. Instead, after a few hours, I'd beg off, go home, and go to bed. I could sleep during the day, but at night I struggled. I found myself drinking about three bottles of Scotch a week, just to help me sleep at night. And I had to admit that I simply couldn't get out of bed at all some mornings. My bedroom became my sanctuary, and at times I found myself uncomfortable outside its four walls.

It was Alex, at eight months pregnant, who finally gave me the push I needed. "For Christ's sake, Nick," she shouted, "have a fucking shower and change your bloody clothes. You stink! Then make an appointment to see the doctor. You're not the brother I had, and my child will have a dirty, lazy, half-pissed guy for an uncle. Get with it and stop feeling fucking sorry for yourself."

I WAS only half aware of the GP Adam Forsythe, a fortysomething man who, according to Mum, was an excellent diagnostician. He seemed to drone on and on from behind his desk as I answered his questions. After about twenty minutes or so, it seemed like I'd been sitting there for a week, but I vaguely understood he'd been thorough.

"So, you've asked me all the clinical questions, including my erectile dysfunction," I said, "and a few regarding my relationship with Rashid Nadar. What now?"

"I'm sorry if I've been intrusive," he said, smiling across his desk. "But you're not here just to fix your erectile dysfunction, as you know. I'm referring you to the best psychiatrist in this town, possibly the whole country. He always gets results of some sort. If he doesn't get people all the way back, he gives them hope and stability again. He needs as much background information as possible so he can focus on each of his patients and give them a 'running start,' as he calls it. With your permission, I'd like to talk to Sophia as well—there's nothing like a mother's perspective in all of this."

I nodded and felt myself actually smile a little; Mum was my one-person ally in all of this. "Once you start with Mum, she'll never stop," I said, surprising myself by smiling again.

I ARRIVED early at Dr. Grover's office and settled myself into a big leather armchair with a stack of magazines on a nearby table. I thumbed through a couple, but nothing interested me, so I tossed them back with a desultory motion, slipping into fucked-in-the-head mode once again. The receptionist smiled at me and said quietly, "Dr. Grover will be a few minutes, Nick. Can I get you a coffee?"

At that moment, the consulting room door opened, and a thirtysomething woman ran out, weeping loudly, thrust her credit card at the receptionist, and then, with increasing volume, sprinted out of the office.

"Dr. Grover will need a few minutes to regroup," the receptionist said, "and you probably need the same. How do you like your coffee?"

"A long black if you have it," I replied, "but I don't drink instant."

"Very sensible," she said with a smile, "like the good doctor."

I'D FINISHED my coffee, which was excellent and seemed to add something to my day, when the consulting room door opened quietly and its occupant walked into the waiting room, holding out his hand.

"My dear young man," he said, "welcome."

"Uhm, thanks," I said. I gasped in shock, and he looked at me with smiling, understanding eyes. Dr. Grover was not of English stock, as I'd thought, but South Asian, wearing a bright maroon-colored turban.

He indicated a comfortable-looking cloth-upholstered armchair, one of a pair, and I sat down, facing him.

"Allow me to set the record straight, dear boy," he said. "I am not a religious person." He pointed to his turban. "In fact, I am an atheist. I wear this out of respect for my culture and tradition. This is most important in your case because the religious dogma that has sent you and your life partner in different directions is well understood by me. I promise you my impartiality, and independence of opinion will be of assistance in helping you readjust to a lifestyle filled with love and kindness, nothing like you are dealing with currently."

"Thank you," I said woodenly, wishing I could put more meaning into my language and expression. "I'm sorry," I went on, "but everything I say these days comes out sounding like I'm not interested, but I do appreciate what you're saying, and if anyone can get me going again, it will be you. I seem to know so."

"Well, thank you, Nick, for your confidence. We both have a task ahead of us, and we have to work together to get the result we want. What is important now is the target we must work toward. So do you have a personal target?"

"I guess my target is simply to get better, throw off this bloody depressive state of mind, and return somehow to the person that I was."

"And how do you think, as a team, we might do that?"

"Well, you tell me. That's why I'm here," I said with a slight degree of exasperation.

"Nick, we have to work toward a situation where you are able to forgive Rashid for what he has done."

I jumped to my feet, eyes blazing, feeling insulted, misunderstood, and abandoned. "Look, Doctor," I shouted.

"Call me Sam. It's easier," he said calmly.

"That bastard has ruined the life we had together and completely fucked my life into the bargain. I can never, ever forgive him. He's been so devious and dishonest, and he made me feel like a fucking idiot which I probably am."

"He hurt you badly, didn't he?" Sam said.

"Of course," I snapped.

"Then together we must find a way to undo that hurt by retracing your steps in time, understanding why he did this, and trying to see his point of view. Then and only then, I suspect, can we get you back to where you should be."

CHAPTER 43
FINDING MY WAY

DR. GROVER prescribed a "medium" dose of a well-known antianxiety medication with instructions to take the bloody things every morning without fail and not to double up if I forgot a dose.

"Put them beside your bed," he said, "and make this the first new routine of your new life. It sometimes takes a lifetime to establish routine in a human's life, but it can be undone in a split second after a life-changing event such as your relationship breakdown. Give the medication a few days to settle your anxiety down, then focus on your routine every day. It doesn't matter if you replicate a routine from one day to another. That's good, in fact. It gives you a foundation to build your new life on."

I thought about the routines in my life, and grudgingly, I had to admit he was correct. "I can get out of bed around the same time," I said, "but I'm hardly working. I get tired and go home early."

"Well, start by going to work around the same time," Dr. Grover said.

"Well, I don't really have a job," I said. "It's a family company, so I can do as much as I want or nothing at all."

"Nick, please don't sit around and do nothing. Work will keep your brain busy."

I glared at him; he was telling me how to run my life, and I simply wanted to get better. "Won't these bloody pills fix my problems, Doctor?" I snapped, and at almost the same time I regretted my words.

"Nick, the medication is purely to calm your anxious state, which is quite obvious. You've been terribly hurt emotionally, and your natural response has been to curl up in bed, keep the world away, and eat and drink to excess to compensate. Then when you look in the mirror and find your beautiful face is blotchy, your tummy bulging, those things make you feel more depressed over and over again. Getting started on routines, diet, exercise—that's the hardest part. Once you get everything going, you'll be surprised how it all comes together. But we have to slow you down first, make a quiet space around you, and that's what the medication is for."

IT WAS about a week later when I started to feel a little better. The days sometimes had a little glimmer of things to look forward to. Not every day, but some days compared to a whole lot of nothing a few months ago. Max and Val were always a nice distraction, and at least once a week I was there for a meal. It was always the same pattern—a Scotch or two, some seafood as an entrée, and usually roast beef or lamb from their freezer. I recognized one of Dr. Grover's routines that made me feel a little more part of a real-life situation, and Max and Val seemed to understand my mindset.

"When we lost Stuart, our reaction was so similar," Val explained. "When such an integral part of one's life is removed in an instant, the human brain retreats in shock, and it takes time, sweetheart, to join the human race once again. We were like zombies for months, but you and your family came along, and we healed, finally. You will heal in time, love, and while you'll think me mad and perhaps a little direct and even heartless, Max and I want to remain fit enough to dance at your wedding."

I looked at them in amazement; the words were caught in my throat, and I was literally speechless.

"Not to that sodding wastrel from Chennai," she said, "but someone nearby, perhaps. Hopefully with similar interests to you, particularly your love of the land, which we believe is a large part of who you are, sweetheart."

CHAPTER 44
A NEW LIFE

IT WAS around five in the afternoon, and Mum, Alex, and I were having a late coffee around the kitchen table when Alex swore like a trooper. She was huge, and only a week away from her due date.

"Fuck!" she yelled. "My water's broken."

Mum, the ever practical one, grabbed dry towels and ushered her into the shower. We made her comfortable, but only a few minutes later, she began groaning. "Now I know what labor pain feels like," she said.

"Be patient, dear. The early contractions can be a shock," Mum said. "I'm afraid you've several hours of hard work ahead, but let's not leave it too long before we get you to hospital, particularly if you have pain."

About 10:00 p.m. I was reading online with my eyes on the screen and my ears pricked up for any progress. Suddenly, doors were banging, lights were switched on, and I could hear Wayne's voice—not strong and authoritative as normal, but plaintive and halting.

"What's going on?" I asked, staring at Wayne, who looked like a confused schoolboy.

"My husband can't cope," Alex said. She gave a curse as another contraction hit her. "I've been in labor for nearly five hours, and the contractions are now five minutes apart. I think I should go to hospital—now," she said with certainty, and quite amazingly, part of my old self kicked in.

"Mum," I said, "ring the hospital and tell them she's on the way. Where's your bag?" I asked, and she pointed to the top of the chest of drawers. I flew out the door as another contraction hit and nearly ran into Wayne. "Help her to dress. I'll get the car," I said as Wayne looked on in wonder. "Bloody come on," I roared, "the contractions are so close she could drop it in the kitchen."

Mum held on to Alex in the back seat while Wayne was in a state of total collapse in the passenger seat. I drove carefully but quickly, mindful of the drugs in my system, and within twenty minutes, Alex was in a birthing suite.

"Christ," said the midwife, a tall slim lady, "another pregnant husband. So how are you doing, pet?" she said to Wayne. "You want something to help you with the pain?"

Wayne put his hand over his mouth and ran for the door. "On your right." She laughed and turned her attention to Alex.

"We'd best leave you," I said, "so you can get on with the job."

"Bullshit," Alex said. "I want you and Mum here, and my silly bloody husband if he can stand the strain." She giggled, then yelled as another contraction signaled the baby was definitely on its journey.

The midwife moved us away and administered a shot of morphine just as Wayne reappeared, looking sheepish. I cuddled him, which seemed to settle him down. The three of us made ourselves comfortable in the rather nice lounge area outside, still in partial PPE gear so we could take turns by her bedside.

"Don't go far away, dears," the midwife said. "She's in good, normal labor, and she could surprise us with a quick delivery. I'll call you on this number if it's imminent." She pointed to Wayne's phone. I dictated my number instead, and she smiled. "Oh yes, our poor husband. Get yourself a coffee from the machine, love, and don't be long."

Ninety minutes later Alex gave a mighty push, and a bundle of arms and legs spilled out. Wayne looked at the mess in fear but held it all together.

"Congratulations, family." The midwife smiled as she patted the little one on the back. "You have a very lovely baby daughter." A daughter who roared her head off. "See," said the midwife, "perfect lungs."

Alex held her precious bundle on her chest after the midwife dried her off. She was my niece, Mum's grandchild, Wayne and Alex's daughter. Mum and I were bleary-eyed but in control as we watched the new addition to our family set about feeding vigorously twenty minutes later. Sometime after that the tears flowed down Wayne's cheeks as he held his sleeping daughter for the first time.

"So, what's her name to be, darlings?" Mum said.

Alex looked at me and smiled, as did Wayne. "Nicole Sophia Edwards," they repeated together, and I couldn't believe my ears. I now had two kids named after me.

CHAPTER 45
DARK DAYS

I SEEMED to fall off a cliff after Nicole was born. The call to action wasn't required once Alex was home from the hospital, because Wayne naturally took over as husband and father. But it was only a matter of a week or so before he needed to escape house and home, and Alex encouraged him.

I sat at the kitchen table with Mum—it seemed to be our official meeting place these days—with a plate of pakoras and beautiful rich coffee.

"How's it all going dear?" Mum asked, sensing I had something on my mind.

"Wayne is bored shitless now Alex is on her feet and there isn't enough work around here for two of us with the subdivision site stuff nearly finished. There's only the marketing after that, so I feel like a useless third wheel."

"But what about Max and Val's property, which we're still leasing. Surely that will keep you occupied."

"Mum, we sold off most of the stock, remember? Only a few head of cattle left, which keeps the feed down and very easy to manage. A few hours a week, that's all it needs to make sure their water and feed's okay."

"Well, the extensions to this place," she said, meaning the hostel, "that needs management, and that's going to be a challenge. That's right up your alley, dear."

I LOVED my mother. She had always been my confidant, my supporter, but I don't think it registered with her that I'd run out of options again. I felt myself slipping back into my own little world. The routines that Sam Grover had spoken of now began to imprison my mind. I had times and places to be, but I didn't want to go there. In fact, my bedroom and office became my only safe and sure environment, and I spent more time there because I didn't have to make decisions or to lead the tribe. Wayne was doing an excellent job, and I wasn't interested. I'd help Wayne get started on a job, then usually by midafternoon I'd disappear to my room and have a nap. I'd started to dream again, and they were all unpleasant. Mostly flashbacks where I'd done something fucking awful and really fucked up. I could see Dad and all the Murphy family, Uncle Robert and Aunt Anne— Bitchface in my dreams— like a horror movie. I felt my existence was aimless again, like when I dumped Rashid for his deceptiveness and duplicity. I looked at some online porn one afternoon, but my poor penis was still in shock, no sign of an erection, in fact it was bloody sore where I'd tried to get it hard. Sam Grover had been sending me emails because I'd missed two appointments, but apart from a dick that wasn't interested, there was nothing wrong with me, so I didn't reply.

All Sam wanted me to do was to fucking forgive Rashid, for Christ's sake, and that simply wasn't on. He could go ahead and ruin some other prick's life; I wasn't going to make it any easier, and I didn't need him where I was going.

Mum, Wayne, and Alex were all pissed off at me again, which was okay. I didn't have to please anyone but myself, and I didn't care anyway. Life wasn't entertaining; it was boring as shit. I missed meals because I didn't feel like eating, it was a waste of time. To keep my sister happy I showered most days, made an appearance, then disappeared back to my bedroom sanctuary. I could tell Mum was upset, but changed the subject when she asked me to go back to Sam Grover.

I was out of antianxiety shit, so I reckoned I certainly didn't need the fucking pills anymore. I cleaned out the old metal garage near the front door of the hostel, which we'd used as a storehouse, because Mum had been pleading with me to do it for a month. It had to be pulled down, but there was a lot of stuff there from Brookside, so I made a point of transferring it under cover in the barn. I cleaned it out, blocked up the gaps underneath, and went in to dinner, which tasted like shit because Alex cooked it and brought it along. It was warmed up, and the five of us sat around the table like old times. Nicole looked really good. I hoped she'd be a better person than the bloke she was named after.

I tried to act as normal as they wanted me to be, kissed everyone good night, including Mum, and went to bed. My alarm went off around midnight, and I got out of bed, the memory of more fucking flashbacks fresh in my mind. I dressed casually and well and quietly tiptoed outside to the old garage, due to be pulled down tomorrow to make way for extensions to the hostel. I pulled the old swing door closed. Unfortunately the lock was broken. I found a bit of rope and tied it in place. That should do the trick, I reasoned. I got into the ute after fitting the flexible pipe to the exhaust, then padded the inlet through the passenger window so it wouldn't leak and started the engine. I settled back, smiling. At least I was able to make a decision for myself this time without other bastards doing it for me. I hoped fucking Rashid would hear about all this shit and know what he'd done to my life.

CHAPTER 46
AFTER THE EVENT

WHITENESS IN front of my eyes—so bright it hurt to open them. Silver pipes and fittings and people in white fucking coats. I had a terrible taste in my mouth. I was in bed, I had a thing on my face like a bloody oxygen mask, and I had a fucking fence around me, like a jail.

"What's this?" I croaked, pointing to the fence.

"That's to stop you rolling out of bed," a male face said. This bloke had a blue gown on and looked like Sam Grover.

"Oh, he's conscious," said a lady who seemed bossy, examining me. "You guys got him out just in time. You said about eight minutes, didn't you?" She was speaking to a woman who sounded like Mum and who was sniffing a lot.

"Yes," she said.

"Okay, watch his oxygen intake on the way and take him downstairs to the hyperbaric chamber," the woman said.

"What if it's in use or booked for treatment?" said another person in a uniform.

"Well tell them fuck off," said the bossy lady. "This bloke needs it more than anyone, and he'll need it off and on for at least three days."

I WAS in this bloody capsule like a submarine, and from time to time I could glimpse people watching me through little portholes in the thing. I slept most of the time, and the experience wasn't all that bad, because I didn't have to worry about anything. They changed my bed linen, gave me a cardboard-looking bottle to pee into, and a nice rubdown to make sure I didn't destroy my circulation and get bed sores, so I was told. I wondered what I was doing here, but every time I tried to think, I slipped off into dreamland again. Pleasant dreams too, mostly with bloody Aaron giving me all sorts of rude hand signals, so that was pretty good. A few days later I was wheeled into a new room; I began to feel hungry and devoured everything in sight and on the menu from which I could order from the bed. This was physical and mental rehab, I was told by the bossy lady, who introduced herself as Pam Smith, the doctor who probably helped bring me back from where I'd been headed.

The full implications began to sink in. I'd tried to end my own bloody life because it all seemed so pointless and because my hatred of Rashid literally drove me to it. When the family walked in, including Aaron, I knew I had some explaining to do. My strength was improving, but I'd already used up today's supply after a regime of exercises designed to keep my mind and body involved at the same time.

I was on the bed with the coverlet over me when Sam Grover walked in. I did feel a degree of guilt, but, as I'd explained to him, over and over, I wasn't about to let Rashid off the hook. That remained the sticking point in my attitude, but as Sam said, "Don't expect the world to agree with you. Your mind will not heal itself until *you* take charge, grow a bigger set of balls, and be strong enough to forgive him. *That* action would immediately make you stronger than him. You would have taken the initiative. You could then laugh at him, walk away from what he's done to you, and resume a normal life. *You* would then be in control, not the other way around. Attempted suicide is a cry for help, but it's also self-indulgent, Nick. You were very fortunate your friends and family were watching out for you."

I looked at them all, and I had an epiphany of sorts. I'd let everyone down by being selfish. I knew it was up to me to get my life in order, but to be honest I didn't have a clue how to do it. It was Aaron who came up with a plan, his practical nature always at the ready.

"Why don't you come home with me for a few weeks," he said. "We've got the hay and silage season coming up, and we can't seem to keep anyone on the payroll for more than a few bloody days. Mum and Dad are so determined, they'll come down here themselves and bloody drag you back, because we all bloody love you, dickhead."

I felt even worse because Aaron's voice broke with the emotion of it all, and I knew I'd let him down more than anyone else, even Mum, who was looking at me through a constant waterfall of tears. I was about to reply when Aaron started up again. Even Alex was silent for once, nursing Nicole while Wayne looked on, stunned.

"One of your problems, Nicky babes, is that you had to leave farming to look after Rashid and the Covid job in India. With him out of the picture, and the subdivision doing so well with Wayne's hard work, your talents were wasted, because you're a better farmer than any of us." Aaron looked me deep in the eyes. "They're Dad's words actually, and he said to tell you we need bloody help."

"How could I refuse," I said with a smile for once. I'd been a really sour-faced bastard for such a long time, and this arrangement was, I suspected, highly suitable for all parties. "When would you like me to come down?" I said.

"This arvo," he said, smiling. "I'm driving. Mum's got tea on the go already. We need to get your gear and stuff, and we'll be off."

"I don't think it's that simple, Aaron," Sam Grover said. "As admirable an idea as it is. I'll need to talk to Pam Smith, the clinician. We must keep a watchful eye on his condition—he could regress if the medication disagrees with him."

"Sam, you've done a great job with Nick, and we all appreciate that. But, Sam, he's coming home with me this afternoon, and I'm taking responsibility for him. So please tell Dr. Smith we think his rehab should go in a different direction."

CHAPTER 47
THE MURPHY EFFECT

WE DROVE through the gate of Carrick, the Murphy's property, at 5:00 p.m. I smiled at Ted, who strode out of the big shed and opened the door for me.

"Welcome home," he said, arms around me as Bernice ran over.

"What about me," said Aaron. "I only bloody live here."

We all laughed at each other with that natural humor that had never gone away, and even in my semidrugged state, it was comforting. As a family group, they worked together so well, they instinctively knew what to do when, and today was no exception. Bernie returned to the kitchen where an appetizing smell filled the house. Ted finished up in the shed, cleaning the grease from his hands while Aaron lugged most of my gear inside, leaving me following like a puppy with the remainder. "Where do you want to sleep, in with me or in the spare bedroom?" he asked politely.

"Spare bedroom," I replied. "You might try to molest me during the night, bitch."

"Don't worry. The lock is rooted on that door. I might start sleepwalking. Anything could happen."

We laughed at each other, so comfortable in our insulting way. This was us saying "I like you." Other people would probably be horrified, thinking we were about to resort to fisticuffs.

The truth was, Aaron and I had often slept together as kids, even after I came out, but something had changed in recent times, and I didn't trust myself. Getting hurt by crushing on my best mate would only lead to having my heart broken again, and I couldn't afford that.

"You've got two people who're waiting to see you," Aaron said. "This way, and we'd better be quiet with this one."

We tiptoed down the hall to Aaron's room. There in his cot was Nicky Jr., sound asleep with his thumb in his mouth and clutching his favorite teddy bear to his breast.

"That's Pooh bear," Aaron whispered. "I read him all A.A. Milne's stuff, and he loves it."

It ran through my mind how Aaron had educated himself so well outside of school and how extensive was his knowledge of all things: from kids' literature written in gentler times, to engineering, art, politics, the environment, etc., etc. He'd bullied his parents to have a small television set in the kitchen so he could watch the *ABC News* channel at breakfast and lunch.

My reverie was broken by him steering me out of the bedroom toward the back door. He opened it, and through the screen door I could see moving shapes in the twilight that came into focus when he turned on the outside light. The kelpies! Maude was there with one remaining pup, a female which I'd already claimed as my own.

"That's Barney," said Aaron pointing to the other big dog. They'd needed an extra dog as Maude had been busily breeding. "And this little sheila is yours, Nick, to replace Rusty. What are you going to call her?"

"Sheila sounds good to me."

"Well, that's excellent because I've been calling her that and now it's official."

Sheila was a beautiful black-and-tan kelpie with straight ears, an elegant head, and a face that made her look like she was smiling all the time. Experience told me she'd be smaller than average, but judging by her lively demeanor, she was never going to be a shrinking violet. I spoke to her, and she sized me up—one of those dogs who while wagging her tail, wagged her entire body.

"Sheila," I said, "I think you're a beautiful girl." Something told me to hold out my arms, which I did, and she leapt off the ground and into my grasp, licking me all over as if I were an ice cream. She settled down, allowing me to cradle her like a baby.

"See," said Aaron. "I told you she was perfect. She's picked you because she's a smart girl."

We moved into the kitchen, where dear Bernie served up a three-course meal I struggled to eat. But something told me to simply enjoy, and I did. I helped clear the table, but weariness overcame me, and I began yawning.

"Shower and bed," Ted said, "you've had a big day, mate."

I tried to protest, but Aaron was unpacking my stuff and directed me to his own ensuite in "his quarters" as he put it. All clean, I smiled my gratitude, rolled into bed, and was asleep before my head hit the pillow.

I had beautiful dreams of my mad mate Aaron, of Sheila, and even Nicky Jr. Ted and Bernie were there in the background, and finally my dad came to visit, and I cried out loud. I started to settle down again when there was a figure beside the bed.

"Are you all right, darling?" he said, and I knew it was Aaron.

"Mmm," I mumbled, pretending to be deeper asleep than I was.

If he wants to call me darling, why not enjoy it.

CHAPTER 48
THE FIRST DAY OF THE REST OF MY LIFE

I WOKE up when I heard one of the tractors start up and immediately felt guilty. I knew the Murphy family didn't expect me to pay for board and lodging, but there was an expectation I'd help them with the harvest season in about two months. So, I had to get myself fit enough to last a ten-hour day, at least, even though I knew it was a ploy on Aaron's part to get me out of the hospital. But it was now up to me to assist in any way I could. I could manage about six hours from waking up to lie down and rest, so I had to do something about it.

Bernie had a huge breakfast cooked, complete with entertainment—Nicky Jr. in his highchair. Nicky had no knowledge of silly people trying to end their own lives. Like all the Murphy family, he seemed to love me unconditionally. He wanted me to lift him down, but he hadn't finished his brekky. So, I pointed to it, picked some up and ate it myself, and he got the message.

"How did you do that?" Bernie asked. "The little bugger is very determined and won't eat properly at all some days, then whinges because he's hungry between meals."

"Dad did the same thing to me, and to Alex," I said, "but Alex worked around him. I was more compliant." Bernie laughed from within; she always saw the world through a sense of humor. "I'll help you with him, Bernie, particularly until I'm physically fit again. But can you mind him for about an hour? There's something I need to do."

"What's that, dear boy?"

"Straighten the front gate where someone's hit it, put it back on its hinges, and clean up the long grass that makes the place look like an Amish settlement."

Bernie roared again, and Nicky Jr. giggled at her. Within the hour I had the job done, slashed then mowed around the entrance to the farm, and used weed killer to keep it neat for a while. Then I cleaned myself up thoroughly, put Nicky in his stroller with the big wheels especially made for rough roads, and off we went for a walk. But we weren't alone. I found a choker chain for Sheila and began her training, teaching her to walk at heel and to sit when commanded. Every time she made the correct response, she was rewarded with a piece of dog biscuit. She was really intelligent, and she had, I realized, a most loving nature for a dog. I watched her interact with Nicky Jr., and it was a case of learning things together. At one stage, they both turned and looked at me together, waiting for the next instruction! I took Sheila off the chain, and it was as if she'd been a working dog forever. She watched, listened, and obeyed. Nicky Jr. wasn't far behind. He started making little whining noises and needed to have a wee. I took him out of the pusher, still in nappies, unpinned them, and he held on, finally letting go a huge torrent. I looked around and laughed as Sheila decided it was her turn also. She squatted next to the stroller, looking for approval!

We came down the hill, Sheila walking sedately at heel and Nicky Jr. laughing his head off. Ted and Aaron looked amazed, but I felt pleased with myself.

"Some people have an easy life," snipped Aaron, but Ted grinned. "The front gate looks terrific. Thanks, Nick," he said. "We get used to things the way they are and don't worry about them. You'll have us dressed in a collar and tie next. I have a feeling we might have to pull our finger out."

Aaron looked mystified. He'd been working up the back fencing and hadn't noticed. Ted waved his hand and Aaron trotted over. The look on his face as he swung the gate to make sure it locked was priceless. He pushed it open again, carefully pulling the latch over. He trotted back and enveloped me in a huge hug.

"You should be resting, you silly tart. But thanks, that makes us feel better, doesn't it, Da?"

"You'll look good in a three-piece suit on the harvester," Ted said as we walked in for lunch. I grabbed Nicky Jr. because he was making dreadful smells.

"Hang on, mate," I said desperately, and the little fellow did, I found his little enamel pot, whipped off the nappy, and he bloody nearly filled it. After I cleaned him up, powdered his bum, and gave him a new nappy, it was time for lunch. Ted and Aaron were already eating because they had to get back to work. Bernie had mixed up the little fellow's veggie-mix baby food, and I started feeding him.

"Nick, leave him. I'll feed him—you've done enough," Bernie said, her eyes sparkling as the little fellow tore into his tucker.

"Look at him go," Ted said, I've never seen him eat like that."

"Little man has had a busy day," Bernie said, "but I reckon he'll go out like a light shortly."

"Someone else needs to do the same thing," Aaron said in a tone that brooked no argument, and I agreed and carried Nicky Jr. into his cot. I wheeled it into my room so I could watch him as Bernie needed to go shopping. Finally, I went out the back, told Sheila to have a pee, and thought to myself that someone or something in the universe was helping. I found her bed, beautiful clean blankets that Bernie laundered weekly, and began to carry it inside. Sheila ran to the other side of the garden and squatted, then presented herself at the door! When Bernie looked in the room, Nicky Jr. and I were snoring and Sheila was curled up in her bed, tail thumping but certainly guarding us against all unimaginable monsters.

CHAPTER 49
PHYSICALITY AND MENTAL HEALTH

AFTER A few days, it dawned on me I hadn't had a negative thought since I arrived, and I realized I'd kept myself as busy as my poor tortured body allowed me. Which demonstrated the connection between physical and mental health. I found an old alarm clock, and despite protestations from Aaron, I set it for six thirty in the morning and made sure I was out and about before the remainder of the family. Aaron tried to scold me, but I had a bout of temporary deafness, so he gave up. I even cooked breakfast some days and ever so slowly began to improve, my body responding.

Aaron dug out his old gym equipment, and I found a corner of the shed with a concrete floor to work out, with Nicky Jr. watching from his stroller and Sheila trembling with excitement at my strange behavior. I knew what she wanted; the genetics of herding are in kelpies, and she needed to be taught to work properly. I grabbed Bernie, and she wheeled the stroller, complete with a slightly uncooperative Nicky Jr., because I wasn't wheeling him.

"Do you understand what's happening here?" Bernie asked.

"No, love, what's happening?"

"This child has bonded to you. He looks for you every moment. He won't even crap unless you're there, he's eating like a horse, and I thought he was a finicky eater! You've done more for this little fella than anyone, including his father."

"Oh, Bernie, I hope I haven't overstepped the mark, have I?" I said, feeling like shit that perhaps my mate's lovely little boy would prefer me to Aaron.

"Nick, Aaron is delighted because he sees Nicky Jr. helping you as well as you are helping him. And the workload has eased on all of us as a family. You're a bloody godsend."

"But what about Ellen Hampstead, his mother, isn't she interested?"

"I don't know, love. You'd better ask Aaron."

We reached the little paddock behind the homestead where about twenty sheep were grazing, most of them meant for the table. I kept Sheila at heel and walked around the flank of the little mob, pushing them gently into a corner. She kept staring at me, but I said nothing as I walked back to Bernie and Nicky Jr.

She sat crouched on the ground, staring at me.

"Now Sheila, get away out there," I said, swinging my arm in one direction. She tore off but slowed just before the mob looked back at me.

"Get away back," I said, rolling my arm in a semicircle, and she ran behind the mob, which started to move toward me.

"Now sit," I said, and she did exactly that, waiting for my further instructions. I was in the front of the mob now and using both hands, beckoning toward myself I said, "Now bring 'em on," and walked off, the sheep following and Sheila behind them. It was all about bringing the sheep to me, and she understood. Most dogs of her tender age were too rough, too fast, and too hard on the sheep, but Sheila was gentle and very much in command. It was then I knew I had a champion dog. No way was she being sterilized—she would make wonderful breeding stock. There was a clapping noise from the other fence where Aaron and Ted were standing, Ted with his mouth open.

"Well, I'll be buggered," Ted said. "I've never seen anything like that before. What's your secret, Nick?"

I didn't have time to answer—because Aaron cut in, "Da, we're just mugs at this game. He's a bloody natural. We should give up and let him train us."

"Too many bad habits," I said with a smirk.

CHAPTER 50
THE UNSPOKEN

IT HAD been at the back of my mind since the Murphy family took me in. I talked to Mum almost every day, and both of us felt a get-together was overdue. With Aaron's help we spoke to Southwest Canola, the owners of Brookside, our old property in which so much of my young life had been invested.

Mum, Wayne, Alex, and Nicole arrived just after 10:30 a.m. in their new vehicle, a beautiful-looking Mazda SUV. For the first time since I tried to depart from this world, I thought about my future transport needs. I hadn't left this place, and if I did, I knew I could always borrow a vehicle if I needed to. With my permission, Mum had sold my old ute; it went for scrap because it had nearly killed someone, and everyone knew that. It was gone, thank heavens, and it certainly appeared the Murphy family had pushed me along far beyond thoughts of ever attempting that again. I was much happier, I was entertained daily by Nicky Jr. and Sheila, and the Murphy family made no secret that they loved me and knew I was stable and even content.

Mum and I went for a quiet walk. I thought she would be upset that I appeared to be enjoying life here rather than at home with her, Alex, Wayne, and Nicole.

"I always worried that I'd dragged you away from your first love, the land," she said, "and here you are, back where you belong. I want you to be happy, dear," she went on. "You were correct that the six hundred acres we're leasing from Max and Val doesn't have any future for farming of any sort. We've hardly had any rain this year, and the feed situation is awful. Wayne has sold off most of the stock, so we're not in any trouble financially."

"I feel guilty I haven't seen Max and Val," I said, "but I've been concentrating on getting my body and my head right—in that order."

"I know, dear, and once again, you have your priorities sorted out, which tells me you're as near to being well again as you probably will ever be. As a matter of fact, Max and Val would like to catch up as soon as possible, and they asked if you'd bring Aaron with you." Mum paused, looking reflective. "I think they want you to buy the entire property from them so their daughter can't get involved after they pass away."

I smiled at Mum; I knew there was more to it. "So let me guess, Mum, the six hundred acres could be a whole new subdivision. It would give us all a lovely income for the foreseeable future—and our Wayne would be brilliant in running it. Probably call it Williams Ridge, am I right?"

"Actually, Williams Heights, because almost every block will have a view."

"Sounds good, and our Wayne is still developing. He's amazing."

"Yes, dear. You haven't lost any of your insightfulness, have you? I also think Wayne is becoming increasingly capable, but he tells everyone that he probably married the wrong Williams kid! Oh God, does our Alex get wound up!"

We laughed like old times, mother and son reunited. Mum cried, and I cuddled her. "I suppose I'll need to come up for board meetings," I said, and she nodded. "We could do the business with Max and Val, hold the board meeting, and load up more of my stuff. I don't know how long the Murphy family can put up with me, but they'll have to throw me out to get rid of me."

We climbed into Ted's Land Cruiser, with Wayne following. We stopped at our old house, and a nice-looking young bloke came to the gate. "The boss rang me and said I was to give you blokes unlimited access, his words. I'm Jacob, by the way. Follow me. The road has changed a bit from when you guys were here."

He led us down the track by the creek in the firm's big Chinese ute, and I was amazed at the sight ahead. Not only had the track been rebuilt but an enormous concrete wall had been built to hold the bank of the creek together. We parked almost on the spot where Dad had died and exited the vehicles in a sober manner. I remembered my manners, and Mum smiled gratefully at me as I introduced us.

"I'm Nick, this is Sophia, my mother, my sister, Alex, her husband, Wayne, and little Nicole." And Aaron introduced the Murphy clan. "Dad may have passed away here, Jacob, but don't ever be reluctant to come down here. He's at peace, and he'll help you rather than hinder you."

"Thanks, mate," he said. "That makes me feel better. I'll leave you guys to it. Call in as you leave—I'd like you to meet my partner, Sarah."

"Now," I said, "Mum, you're first."

One by one, each of us took a silver cup of Dad's ashes and cast them along the edge of the creek. We stood around and talked about him and the farm and what had happened since, and in particular how my journey had brought me back again, albeit over the road with the Murphy family.

Wayne was strangely silent, and Aaron and I guessed why at the same moment.

"It's all right, Wayne. You didn't know Dad, but he would have loved you," I said, and Aaron chipped in.

"Yeah," he said drily, "any poor bastard who could put up with his daughter would be a hero in his eyes!"

Even Mum laughed. It was exactly the right comment at the right time as Alex launched a stream of invectives that would make a shearer blush.

Ted, however, was inconsolable. He sobbed and sobbed, and we all held him.

"Thanks, guys," he said, "but this is really the first time I've had to grieve. He was my best mate, and I miss him terribly, every day. We are two families from very different bloodlines and beliefs, yet we are always in each other's minds. Right now, Trevor Williams would rest easy if we were to have a bloody good party. And let's make sure the young manager and his missus are invited.

"Your dad still visits me. I'm Irish and those close to us stay close even though they've passed on. I believe he comes back from time to time to sticky beak, watching how we're going. He's here with us now, but ever since Nick has come to live with us, I can tell you he's happier than a pig in shit. Now let's go over the road. There's plenty of beds if you want to stay the night, because my demeanor is bein' influenced by the thought of a nice glass of red wine."

CHAPTER 51
READY FOR HARVESTING

TALKING TO Ted and Aaron about getting ready for harvesting was like pissing into the wind. I looked at the machinery in the barn and couldn't stand it any longer.

"We don't need any breakdowns during the harvest," I emphasized, "particularly as November can be weather sensitive for hay."

"It'll be right, mate," Aaron said. "Plenty of time, so why don't you go and have a rest this arvo. We'll get to it next week."

I lost it. "No, Aaron. Drag that shit out where I can work on it, now, please."

He looked at me, a touch cross, but I think he remembered our two families still held fifty percent each of the two balers, and we'd never called in our share after selling up Brookside and leaving. The state-of-the-art mower was only a season old, and fully owned by the Murphy family, so after a cursory inspection, I left it alone.

Finally, Aaron dragged the round silage baler out into daylight. I told him to leave the big tractor on it while I ran it up. I asked Bernie to watch both Nicky Jr. and Sheila, because it could be dangerous. I connected the power take-off, let in the clutch, and the baler began to spin. There was an audible knocking sound coming from the rear. I watched, and sure enough, an actuator shaft wasn't running as smoothly as it should. And the heavy-duty pickup for the green forage was also shaking quite violently. I stopped the machine, turned off the tractor, and just looked at Aaron.

"How long has this been going on?" I said.

"Look, to be honest, the last day of baling, I didn't take much notice because it still worked all right, and I was worried about you."

I had to laugh at him then, standing there like a naughty schoolboy, knowing he was in the shit and trying to get out of it. "Well at least you washed it down before you put it away. That'll keep most of the grit out of the bearings."

Ted came along as we stripped the problem shaft of its bearing in the delivery chute and then straightened the pickup mechanism cold, finding one of the major support bearings was ruined. It took an hour with a bearing puller to remove it.

"Jesus, yer old man would kick my arse if he saw that, mate. I suppose we'd better order some new parts," Ted said.

"I haven't looked at the square baler yet, and that's nearly as old as me, so you'd better hold your fire."

Ted paled. We were closing in on the harvest season, and the square baler needed everything bone dry before baling, but the round baler could start as soon as the crop was ready.

We pulled out the antique baler, and I could see the grease gun and the baler hadn't been close friends. By this stage both Ted and Aaron were stepping around as if on eggshells, trying to look as if they were invisible. I greased every nipple and started the old thing up. Miraculously, it seemed to be fine. I couldn't find anything out of place, but I found the old, tattered handbook and checked all the adjustments, tightening a few of them.

Bernie called out that lunch was ready, and I was hungry again. I'd been a bit self-indulgent this morning, stepping on the scales to find I was nearly my old weight again but much improved musculature, which meant I was probably better physically, if not yet mentally, after my stupidity.

Aaron and I hopped into his crew-cab ute and drove into town. The parts weren't on the shelf, as I'd expected, but would be available in two days. When I enquired about the pickup mechanism parts, the manager rolled his eyes.

"I've got a complete unit back there that a bloke cancelled on me. I'd give it to ya at half price."

"Done," I said, and Aaron's eyes widened. We carefully lifted the unit, still in its crate, with the help of the dealer's forklift, leaving the tailgate down with a piece of rag on it to comply with the law.

"FEEL LIKE a cup of coffee?" Aaron said, and I nodded. We left our vehicle parked outside and walked down the main street, taking in the changes that really neither of us had noticed since the pandemic. Restaurants in particular had fared badly; several had closed up and never reopened.

"Christ, this part is like a bloody ghost town," Aaron said, as he took my hand. I was well accustomed to Aaron demonstrating affection, but in my memory, this was the first time he'd ever done so in public. "I told ya I'd walk down the bloody street holdin' yer hand, and I don't think you believed me." He grinned. "Something about who we might meet up, like yer Uncle Robert."

We nearly wet our pants when, with immaculate timing, who should be not a hundred meters away but the man himself. Uncle Robert was a bit stooped over and had a quite attractive teenage girl with him.

"Uncle Robert," I said as they neared us.

"Why, Nick, my dear boy, how lovely. And young Aaron, isn't it? Oh, how nice to see you both."

In very uncharacteristic behavior, Uncle Robert threw his arms around me and then did the same to Aaron. "I heard about all your troubles, Nick, and how Aaron and his family took you in. I must say you look wonderful!"

"I am, thanks, but who's this?" I said, pointing to the girl. I knew the older kids: Richard the mad masturbator, Amanda who had allowed the entire male population in for tea and toast, then Danny and Gillian, the youngest.

"This is Danielle," Uncle Robert said proudly, "and she is transitioning."

I suddenly realized Danielle had been Danny, but Aaron wasn't quite with it yet. A few more minutes and I knew he'd line up everything, and that would be cool, but in the meantime his mouth hung open like a large front-end loader.

"We were just going for a coffee. It's been a while since lunch, why don't you join us?" I said.

"Oh, that would be lovely, boys. The bakery over there has some really beautiful food and the best coffee ever."

We ordered, and Aaron's front-end loader finally snapped shut and he was on board. "Gosh, you're really pretty, Danielle. Are there any other trans kids in town?"

I squirmed in my seat, but Danielle took it in her stride. "Yes, there are two others we know of and a third who's too frightened to come out."

"You might say we've had a struggle, boys, but I'm not sorry. Thanks to Danielle I'm personally in a better place. When Danielle confided in us, as she was trained to do, Anne went crazy. Her religious beliefs have, I think, led her to be possessed by religious mania. She wanted to hold an exorcism to rid my girl of the so-called devil inside her. When she wouldn't allow Danielle in the family home, I left, taking Danielle with me. We're renting here in the town, and I go out to the farm during the day. Fancy rejecting your own child," Uncle Robert said. "She even called a meeting of the church committee and had me removed because I'd set a bad example! Looking after our own child!"

The coffee and buns arrived, and we tucked in, delicious country tucker baked that morning. I bought a big bag to take home.

Aaron wasn't finished, however. "Robert, you said you were in a better place, yet everything is completely topsy-turvy in your life, and I can't even imagine the financial stuff when you and Mrs. Williams settle up."

Uncle Robert stared down at his second coffee, thinking. "Having been thrown out of church was the best thing that has ever happened to me. Trevor always worried about the influence of the church on me and wanted me to 'be of independent thought,' and he was right. Anne ran our lives in that regard, the most painful instance being when your father was killed, Nick. I said to Anne I had to leave immediately, but she said I should stay because I was doing God's work, and that Trevor was only a heathen anyway. I have never been so ashamed of myself and that will haunt me forever. But to answer your question, Aaron, I have finally freed myself from religion. I live my life now with pride knowing everything I do is my decision, and if it might happen to be wrong then I have only myself to blame, because God and Jesus can look after themselves now, the bloody hypocrites."

"And where are you living at the moment?"

"In Howard Street, Aaron, but we only have two weeks left. We've been renting by the month, and the owners want to move back in. We'd have to really go bush to find a place, and Danielle would be too far from school. I have to be close to the farm. Anne is unbalanced and won't seek help. To be honest I don't know what to do."

"Whaddya reckon about the old shearer's quarters?" Aaron asked, as if I were the owner.

"Well, I've only really looked inside once," I said, "but it's in really good condition for its age. Electric stove and hot water, nice little kitchen cum lounge, and three bedrooms."

"And the bathroom is huge. You could fit two shearers in the shower." Aaron giggled, and Danielle laughed. Her eyes lit up.

"The school bus goes past the gate, Dad," she said, "and you'd only be twenty minutes from the farm."

"Aaron, what about your parents? What would they say about this?"

"They'll say yes."

CHAPTER 52
A FAMILY FULL OF SURPRISES

UNCLE ROBERT and Danielle clearly thrived on good food, a family atmosphere without stress, and love which came from a surprising source— Ted. He managed to get Uncle Robert well lubricated on red wine most nights, and one night in particular, about a week after they arrived, all the hurt, the guilt, and his rather sad life story came tumbling out. How he met Anne Baxter, a pretty, quite tall, and even a touch elegant girl, and he fell head over heels in love. How Anne's family were a little "churchy," which he went along with, and started attending, later going on to be on the committee. A "born-again" pastor was appointed, and from that point forward, "Anne had been hooked." By the time their last child, Gillian, was born, Uncle Robert was told to find his own bedroom "because that activity was for procreation only."

For Bernie, using the stove in the shearer's quarters was an insult and only allowed at breakfast. She insisted we all sit down together at the dining room table in the homestead. The true meaning of family became clear soon enough. Danielle would exit the bus, change, and begin helping Bernie with the evening meal. Bernie sensed Danielle needed a real mother, and they became close. But there was the future at stake and Danielle had to complete homework before she helped with culinary duties.

One Friday night—after we'd done a solid day's harvesting, Uncle Robert had drafted off some fat lambs for sale, and Bernie had done the weekly shopping—Danielle surprised everyone with a three-course dinner. Seafood cocktails to start, roast beef with homemade horseradish sauce, roast veggies, and a huge platter of hot greens, all set out on the big old sideboard as a buffet so we could help ourselves. Bernie was her assistant, amazed at Danielle's competence. For dessert there was fruit trifle. We sat back with bellies bulging.

Bernie just shook her head, amazed. "Danielle, darling, you have enormous capability for cooking and entertaining. That's a real feather in your cap. You should try to do something like that for a living."

"I want to do a proper domestic science degree at university next year and then teach domestic science at schools. But I have to find a place to board in Geelong next year, and that's nearly as difficult as Dad finding a place to live down here. If it hadn't been for you people, we'd be on the street."

I excused myself and rang Mum. "Is my bedroom still unused?" I asked.

"Yes, dear, I kept it open in case you wanted to come home or visit."

"I could always stay with Alex and Wayne."

"What have you got on your mind?" she said abruptly but laughed at the same time.

I explained about Danielle, someone who could work part-time in the kitchen but attend classes during the day. It was perfect. Only nominal board, real wages to help with her studies, and lots of local LGBTIQ+ people to embrace her and care for her well-being, along with Mum, Alex, and Wayne as backstops.

Danielle cried, and it was obvious Uncle Robert was lost for words.

"I think the old Nicholas Williams has returned," said Ted. "I think we should have a glass of red to celebrate."

Uncle Robert was still speechless but raised his glass and then made a speech about the wonders of human life and values, while Bernie even had a glass herself.

"But what about Gillian?" I asked. "What's going to happen to her? I mean, Richard and Amanda have jobs in Melbourne, and Gill must feel as if she's living in a fishbowl."

"I agree, Nick. There's a court order preventing Anne from doing anything, financially or physically, to anyone or anything. Next Monday I go to court seeking temporary custody of Gill."

"She's coming here as well, then," I said, knowing without asking the Murphys would be fine with it. "At least you'll have part of your family around you."

"If we promise to behave, dress nicely, and look like an alternative family, do you think the magistrate would be impressed?" said Aaron.

"Yes, that would be marvelous," Uncle Robert replied. "I've a nice solicitor from Geelong who is representing me and handling the case. We need Anne to submit to a psychological examination, which we believe will show she is unfit to be a parent. The next step will be to have her committed to a private hospital, which is being handled by, ah," he stumbled and blushed, "your psychiatrist, Dr. Grover."

"Good." I grinned. "I'll get him to look me over while he's in town."

CHAPTER 53
THE FAMILY CHANGES AGAIN

IT WENT well; the magistrate was sensible and heard the evidence presented in a well-researched manner by the young lawyer, tracing Uncle Robert and Aunt Anne's marriage and family in chronological order. Aunt Anne sat there with a look of disdain on her face. She wore no makeup and was dressed like an Amish woman, totally in black with a frilled collar. It was clear she thought she was presenting herself as a pious follower of her church. In her mind, her Lord had ultimate authority over the law of the land, and she told the magistrate so.

"Your flim-flam has no place in my business," she said. "The Lord is my only judge in this matter."

The magistrate ignored her, which I thought was a good sign. He asked intelligent questions, including the full story of Danielle's transition, understanding why Uncle Robert left home. Uncle Robert was marvelous explaining how it was unnatural for a mother to reject her child under any circumstances, and that the threats made to Danielle's life had no basis in any real Christian organization, and that's why he'd left home to care for her with the help of the Murphy family. "Who," he said, "are all in court in support of Danielle and myself. I'm terrified that our youngest daughter, Gillian, could also be in physical and certainly mental danger if she continues to live at home with her mother."

It was over. Gillian was located in the church hall being "supervised" by church members. Uncle Robert agreed, under pressure from Bernie, that we'd stay together as a group for a week or so to give Gillian, a bright thirteen-year-old, a family structure with a female figure "running the place," as Bernie said, and no one disagreed with her. Only then would Uncle Robert return with his kids to his own house.

We celebrated again, and Uncle Robert sidled over to me. "I have a spare vehicle at home, Nick, quite surplus to our requirements. If you organize the roadworthy certificate, it's yours, a gift for your loving kindness. Your father would be so proud of you, and I feel duty bound to help you now, as much as I can. Oh, and it's an old Ford Falcon wagon, runs on LPG and petrol, done only forty-five thousand kilometers or thereabouts."

LATE IN the afternoon, Sam Grover arrived, and we sat in my bedroom for privacy.

"You're amazing, Nick," he said. "Look at you!"

We discussed my medication, and I had explicit instructions on how to taper the doses down and how to react if my negative mindset began to reassert itself. We spoke about the land, my obvious connection to it, and the nurturing Murphy family who had claimed me as their own. Sam's eyes twinkled for some reason; I didn't understand why, but I hopped in before he could ask the final question.

"No, Sam, I don't hate Rashid anymore. I feel like an observer now, looking on in a dispassionate way. I actually feel sorry for him that he felt so obligated by his culture that he did what he did. Would I forgive him? Probably, given more time. You were right to measure my recovery in this manner, Sam, and you can add my case to your list of recovered souls. I know I have a way to go yet, but the positive fact is that I know with absolute clarity that I'll never go back to that dark place."

"I agree, dear boy," Sam said with that laughing twinkle in his eye again.

CHAPTER 54
THE TURNING POINT

I'D NEVER known Ted and Bernice to have a holiday, but when they mentioned going to the beach for a few days, I practically pushed them out the door. Bernie insisted Nicky Jr. go with them, and I was appalled.

"Jesus, Bernie, you're supposed to have a holiday, not be a nursemaid to a nearly two-year-old."

Once again, Bernie won. "Nick, you've trained him so well he's no problem. When he begins missing you, we'll head home."

"Jesus, it's us and the dogs," I said to Aaron, who seemed a bit twitchy this morning. I put it down to the fact that he'd worked hard for months on the farm, on me, and everything that made the Murphy family such a successful unit. His parents were growing toward retirement age and yet they were still putting the hours in: on the farm, in the home, and rescuing bloody injured things like me. I knew he worried about them because they didn't seem to have a plan for their retirement years.

"Feel like a walk with the dogs?" He grinned at me.

"Yeah, where are we going?"

"To the old swimming hole."

"Oh, okay," I said, trying not to look too pleased. It was still one of my favorite places in the world. Of all the sophisticated places I'd been to with Rashid, none had lovely memories of this place. Sheila was delighted to be free again. She'd come in season, and I'd locked her in the old woodshed until it was all over. Maude, her mother, tried bossing her around, and Barney, Aaron's dog, did his own thing. We set off with a bottle of water each, and about half an hour later, breathing heavily in the early summer warmth, we breasted the hill and made our way down the back paddock to the pond. Maude and Barney raced into the water, yapping and playing like puppies. Sheila hung back, not quite sure what this water and splashing noise was all about. Aaron had thoughtfully brought an old tennis ball along because Barney was addicted to it. He threw it into the pond, and Barney, swimming like a fish, grabbed it and returned to shore, dropping it in front of us. Sheila watched, trembling but dry. I pointed where to throw it—closer to Sheila. Aaron lobbed it into the water and Sheila took off like a jet, diving under Barney and grabbing the ball. She smiled around the circumference of the ball and dropped it at my feet. We couldn't help but laugh at her, not only was she the cleverest creature I'd ever seen, but she'd just had her first swim and loved it. Barney looked offended and Maude a little surprised.

"Aren't they amazing," I said.

"Like you," he said as his arm gently slipped around my waist, cuddling me from behind, kissing me on the cheek, and resting his chin on my shoulder as he had always done.

Suddenly the dam inside me broke, and I cried. Big sobbing noises, my chest heaving with the effort of my emotions. I'd never shed a tear since Rashid and I split, but now I howled loudly, pouring out all the hurt, anger, and fear I'd collected.

"Let it all out, darling," he said. "This was overdue."

I gradually calmed down, and he kissed me on the cheek again. "Feel any better now?" he asked, his face a picture of compassion.

"I wasn't crying so much because of my problems," I said. "I cried because no person could have a friend like you. You're amazing, Aaron. You've always been there for me, you've saved my life this time, and you've given me some bloody hope for the future." I breathed in deeply, feeling uninhibited because of my emotional outburst. "I'll have to move on soon and give you a chance to spread your wings. It's a pity, I know, but I can't be selfish."

"Waddya talkin' about, ya silly queen."

"Because you're a straight man, and you'll need to settle down with a lady."

"I'm about as straight as a bent stick. We're both playin' for the same team."

"Aaron," I said, "you're the most gentle, beautiful person I know, but now you're verging on being cruel, leading me on. You're straight, for Christ's sake. What about Nicky Jr.?"

"Ellen Hamstead was my surrogate."

I began to feel like an idiot, my blood pressure rising. "But you can't be gay," I said. "And if you are, who else knows?"

"Not a soul except Mum and Dad, and they're sworn to secrecy."

"But why didn't you tell me, for Christ's sake? Why let me go and make an idiot of myself with Rashid?"

"Because at that stage, I didn't know myself. You're one of the lucky people in this world who was born with that knowledge. It was so easy and natural for you."

Intrigued, I felt my anger drain away. "When did you realize the fact?"

"You remember the weekend we had in Melbourne at the gay nightclub?"

I giggled. "Yes, absolutely. You got so pissed we had to carry you home, and anyway, you met Greg again at the airport when you picked me up from the Rashid disaster."

"So, you remember what else happened at the nightclub?"

I knew exactly what he meant and nodded my head. "Yes, you were dared to kiss a bloke, but you said the only bloke you'd ever kiss was me, and you did."

"And what happened after that."

"I got hard, immediately."

"So did I," Aaron said, "but I was in denial. I felt I couldn't be gay, for Christ's sake. Not because I would be ashamed of being that way, but I was bloody flabbergasted. It was like you awoke sumthin' in me. I tried makin' love to as many women that were willing, and it just got worse. Couldn't even get a stiffy, in the end, so I gave it all away. Then I had a few trial runs with blokes, most of 'em useless, but I knew."

"But why didn't you tell me?" I demanded.

"Because by that time you'd moved away to Geelong and met Rashid. I had no business pushing my way in. That was your life, and you deserved some respect. Rashid hated me because he saw me as competition, but it was your happiness in question, and all I could do was back off."

"And when I came home a bloody mess, you looked after me. Why? And why didn't you tell me about your mindset and sexuality back then?"

"Because Blind Freddie could see you were so fragile and vulnerable. Pushing myself onto you might have made you worse. As it was, I nearly lost you," he said, and his voice broke. He sobbed into his hands, reliving his experiences. "That's when I decided to bring you home, and I've been tryin' to get the words out for weeks now, but we've been so busy, and there was always someone around and—"

I flew over, used my hanky to dry his eyes, and before he knew what had happened, I kissed him right on the lips. His arms went around me, and his naughty tongue took over. I stopped and looked down. For the first time in nearly two years, I had an erection—not just any old thing, but one like a randy teenager. And I wasn't the only one. Aaron stood there with a huge bulge, and I went for it, releasing it and taking control. We were in romantic heaven when there was a noise behind us. Three dogs sat side by side making what sounded like a retch. Sheila in particular looking confused, but she was still wagging her tail.

Aaron kissed me again. "What say we go home? It's a lot more comfortable there, and we can lock these bastards outside while we do a bit of exploring."

CHAPTER 55
BEDROOM GYMNASTICS

I THINK all the feelings I'd held for Aaron surfaced at once, and no doubt it was the same for him. We tore inside, our clothing flying everywhere, and landed on his bed. We seemed to love kissing each other, and we didn't seem to be able to stop. At the same time, we tried every position either of us had ever learned from our previous experiences and applied them. There was certainly an "us," and we knew it immediately. Nature is a wonderful thing, and as two fit young blokes who hadn't been sexually active for a while, we went at it.

I lost count of the number of times we made love, but at around four in the afternoon, I staggered into the kitchen and made us coffee. Proper coffee and some nice fruit cake Bernie had made.

"Because we need to keep our strength up," I said to him as he shuffled into the kitchen in his underwear, looking exhausted but with a smile on his face.

"You've bloody worn me out," he agreed, chuckling. "Need a bit of sustenance."

"Listen to who's talking," I said. "I think we're making up for lost time."

"Yeah, are you cool with all of this?"

"Do I look despondent?"

"You look amazin' to me. To be honest I've got to pinch myself to believe this is real, I've bloody dreamt about it, but sometimes I thought it would never happen. I didn't know if you liked me like that. You know."

I put my arms around his hairy being, cuddling him for a change. "So, when I was in India, so far away you thought our paths wouldn't cross for a long time, if ever, that's when you organized Nicky Jr."

"Yeah, and now he's your kid."

"No, ours. Your mum has picked that. He knows which one of us to pump when he wants something."

We laughed. Hardly a day had passed, and we both missed our kid!

I fed the chooks and gathered the eggs while Aaron cooked us a beautiful light dinner, full of protein.

"I think we should have an early night," he said with a twinkle in his eye.

Sheila was distraught, however. She'd been fed with the other dogs and kept tapping on the screen door with her paw for admittance.

"You've ruined that bloody dog," Aaron grumped as I opened the door. I didn't respond because he was probably correct. Sheila made a beeline for the lounge, where the television was featuring a rerun of a "Vera" episode. Sheila settled down on her favorite rug while we cuddled on the couch. Aaron had a shower, so I put Sheila out for a pee. In record time she was back at the door, and I let her in, pointing to the spare bedroom where her bed was located. To my surprise she looked as if she were ill. She arched her back and threw herself down in her bed, glaring at me.

I showered, but there was a man inviting me into his bed, doona rolled back, air-conditioning purring away, and I couldn't resist. I slipped under the covers, and there was a dreadful, mournful noise! Sheila began howling her head off, and Aaron cursed.

"Leave it to me," I said. I went to my old bedroom, picked up her bed, and carried it into our room, throwing it in the corner. She wagged her tail, curled up, and was asleep in seconds.

"Well, I'll be fucked," Aaron said. "What does that mean, Oh Dog Whisperer?"

"She not only likes you, but she also approves."

"Of you having your way with me."

"I suppose she's smarter than I gave her credit for."

I AWOKE just after daylight, cuddled up from behind as was Aaron's custom. But I was also aware of having a wet nose. My nose was being licked by a dog who was smart enough not to wake her greatest detractor but knew I'd wake and let her outside. Which I did. I scurried quietly back to the bedroom, and a voice said in a commanding tone, "Get back into bed. It's Sunday and a day of rest."

"Ah, Father Murphy, shouldn't you be holding Mass this morning with one hand on the Bible and the other where it shouldn't be?" I said.

"Get into bed and I'll read you a sermon. You'll find it very modern in content and not at all confrontational. In fact, I reckon you'd make a good disciple."

We finally struggled out at nine thirty when Aaron's phone rang its funny tune. It was his father.

"No, everything's fine here, the house hasn't burnt down, all the stock have plenty of feed and water, so don't worry. How's Mum and Nicky Jr.?" Aaron laughed. "I thought he might get a bit toey missing you know who."

A brief pause and Aaron went on, "No, Da, you are not coming home under any circumstances, understand? We'll come down and pick him up this arvo. You and Mum need to have a proper break, and two bloody days doesn't qualify. Have you caught any fish yet? Well, bloody get on with it. I'd like a feed of fish tonight. Nick's a ripper fish cook. All right, then, see you about two o'clock. Bye."

CHAPTER 56
THE CAT OUT OF THE BAG

SHEILA LOOKED so disconsolate as we were about to leave that I allowed her to come with us. She sat in the back seat in her own little harness, staring out the window like visiting royalty. We took my Falcon wagon; I'd serviced the old thing, and even Aaron grudgingly admitted it ran so well. We pulled into the car park of the old hotel and led Sheila over to a shady tree with some water. We walked into the dining room and there were Bernie and Ted, having an early afternoon tea with our kid attempting to remove a table leg with his fingers. He was almost walking and certainly talking now. Very advanced, I thought, but who wouldn't be, growing up in the Murphy family. He spotted us and that was it.

"Big," he screamed, which came from Big Nick, and there was no mistaking "Daaaad."

Bernie had him tethered with a safety harness, and he nearly dragged her across the room. He gurgled and cuddled and farted.

"Christ," said Aaron, "have you been feeding him fish?"

"Yes dear, he loves it, and it's so good for him."

We ordered coffee and some cake while I gave him a bottle.

Most men are stupid. Women have intuition as a birthright.

"So, when did this happen?" she said quietly to her son.

"Yesterday," Aaron replied.

Ted looked on with furrowed brows. "What?" he said. "What happened yesterday? Is everything all right on the farm? Are you kids hurt or something?"

"Aaron and Nick are finally together," Bernie said.

Ted stood bolt upright at the table, looking wildly from Aaron to me and back again. Then he shouted out, something between a roar and a cheer, pointing his finger rapidly between the two of us. He sat down promptly in his seat and burst into tears!

"A very Irish male reaction," Bernice said calmly, "and not a bad feature."

CHAPTER 57
TWISTS AND TURNS

I WAS in the barn with the Falcon's back seat folded down and the tailgate open, assessing the available space. A voice came from behind me. "Whattcha doin'?"

"There's a lot of gear I have to move. I don't think this old thing is suitable. I've got to be home in Geelong tomorrow."

"Oh," said Aaron, "when will we see you again?"

"Oh, about six o'clock, I reckon."

I looked at his face, which had turned from downcast to delighted.

"Did you really think for a moment I'd piss off back to Geelong after what we've become?" I asked. I cuddled him, and he laid his head on my shoulder.

"It's all so new," he said, "and sometimes I get panic attacks when you're not around."

"You're a good man, Aaron Murphy. I think for a while we're going through role reversal—I'm the carer now and you're the patient! We should give ourselves twelve months to practice living together so we're constantly in each other's life, and just to be sure my depression is under control. What do you think?"

"How could I disagree?" he said. "Life is amazing at the moment."

"Then why don't we take your big vehicle tomorrow and take Nicky Jr. with us? I've so much stuff I need up here, and your big twin cab is perfect. Max and Val want to talk to us anyway."

"You like my big vehicle," he said suggestively.

"Yes, the way it grunts in the low gears."

MAX AND Val were showing further signs of aging. Neither could walk properly without some sort of assistance, but with everyone helping, they'd been able to stay in their own home. So the welcome was brighter than ever, and I could see the news had traveled faster than we had.

"Just what we wanted to hear," Max said, "for what we have in mind. We want to sell this place, house and land, all on one title, before we cark it, and we all know and understand that's not too far away. We've always loved Nick and his family." Max grabbed Aaron's hand. "No one could have been kinder, and frankly, we wouldn't be around if it hadn't been for their loving care. Nick, in so many ways, has taken the place of our late son. His name was Stuart, and he was a lovely gay man. Things were more difficult back then for gay people, but we worked hard to reassure him and his partner that we loved them." Max paused and then carried on, noting the distress on Aaron's face. "It's okay, Aaron. It was a drunken driver in a car smash—thank heavens it was instant. But the reason I wanted you here, Aaron, was that we nearly lost Nick after the catastrophe caused by a love affair gone wrong."

Aaron put his face in his hands again and quietly sobbed.

"I love to see a man who shows his feelings so openly, Aaron. If it makes you feel any better, it was me that raised the alarm, and they got our lovely boy out in time. Then you took over and look at him now! A credit to both of you. Don't feel that you let the side down, Nick," he said. "I tried something similar after we lost Stuart, but Val knows me inside out. It took me nearly two years of therapy, and she stuck to me, never giving me away for an instant. So, we have lots in common.

"Now, to the business at hand," Max said. "Our daughter, Amelia, is a wealthy woman in her own right."

"My own daughter remains a bitch," Val said, "but Max and I have had enough input into her two kids to ensure they'll make good human beings. So, we've catered for them separately and generously so their parents can't touch their individual legacies. But this house and the three hundred acres need to be disposed of before, as my husband says so eloquently, we cark it."

"Because if we don't, she'll come after the property like the greedy girl she is. So, I reckon about one and a half million," Max said. "What do you reckon?"

"It's worth ten times that as residential land," Aaron said.

"Yes, my boy, but it hasn't yet been rezoned, so speed is of the essence. I'd love to give you the property, but Amelia would then challenge the estate and grab her share. But it's only grazing country now, and the house needs work, so she'd know I'd outfoxed her."

CHAPTER 58
MY REMARKABLE MOTHER

IN MY time away from our core businesses—the hostel and property development—I'd understandably lost touch. Firstly, I was in India running the Stop Covid Forever campaign, then back home with progressively worsening mental illness, and finally my recovery with the Murphy family. Mum knew where I needed to be, which was on Carrick with the Murphy mob, but my money was invested in the family company, and Mum was adamant she needed me to help run the business. So it was agreed I'd make the trip at least twice a month, attending board meetings and being involved in all the important decisions. We sat around the dining room table at a board meeting, and I was blown away. Through an investment company that was paid on results, in a little under three years, Mum had increased cash at hand to an eye-watering amount.

I immediately asked about the tax liabilities, and Mum answered in Swahili, or a language quite similar. Wayne, Alex, and I asked her to elaborate, and the mists began to clear somewhat. It was really quite straightforward. We were exposed to capital gains tax and stamp duties through the property development business.

"However," Mum said, "what would improve our position going forward is the acquisition of more farming property with its myriad of claimable items. Max and Val have offered their remaining property to us through Nick and Aaron for one point five million, which is an average price for a rural house and three hundred acres needing a lot of work. I think we all understand their reason why. This needs to proceed immediately," Mum said, "because the city council is poised to rezone this area from rural residential to residential. At Aaron and Nick's request, a lifetime tenancy agreement on the house and five acres will protect Max and Val. Are we all in favor?"

We nodded our heads, and it was recorded in the minutes kept by Alex.

"Now," Mum said, "Max and Val's property will only offer temporary taxation relief while its purpose is primary production. But I feel we need another rural property with all those lovely deductibles."

"Leave that to me," I said. "I have an idea."

CHAPTER 59
THE NEXT STEP

I WAS quiet on the way home, with Aaron driving. As usual, he read my mind. "So, it's important that we close on Max and Val's place before the next city council meeting, isn't it?"

"Yes, it is, and we will, and that's been decided. You are fifty percent of the offer, so you'll have seven-hundred-and-fifty-thousand-dollars' worth of shares in the Williams family company."

"But I don't have seven hundred and fifty grand in my back pocket. Where's that coming from?"

"If needs be I can loan it to you, but I have an idea that might work for all of us, particularly Ted and Bernie."

"Which is?"

"Acquiring Carrick for the company, with you and I running it and ensuring a proper retirement plan for your parents."

"I'm all ears," Aaron said, and just then Nicky Jr. stirred, uncomfortable because he was probably hungry. I pushed the pacifier into his little gob, and he grinned at me.

I gave Aaron chapter and verse of my proposition as we neared Carrick. Being an intelligent person, a lateral thinker who soaked up information like a sponge, it was easy to paint the picture for him. His questions were still pouring out as we pulled up in the yard. I knew Aaron had a one-third share of Carrick, his parents two-thirds. And it was a fact we were all marking time, none of us sure in which direction we were headed.

So, it was time for a change.

CHAPTER 60
A CLEVER SHEILA

WE DROVE into the yard, and Sheila was waiting at the front gate, overjoyed to see us. As I opened the gate, Nicky Jr. struggled a little, so I sat him down. Sheila put her head down, near his chest, and whimpered to him.

We stood immobile, watching as our child reached up and found her collar. She turned ever so slowly, with Nicky Jr. hanging on tightly, and the pair of them "walked" to the veranda and the front door. There was a hollowed-out sandstone step at the edge of the woodwork, and Nicky Jr. went down slowly onto his knees. Sheila leapt onto the veranda and poked her head toward his chest once again. He giggled and grabbed hold of her collar with both hands as she gently dragged him up and over onto the timber floor.

"I'll never complain about her sleeping inside again, ever," Aaron said with misty eyes. "She's his bloody nursemaid."

"Unfortunately, no one would believe us," I said, a little sorrowfully.

"Prepare for internet meltdown," Aaron said. "I videoed it all."

CHAPTER 61
A NEW ERA

HOW DO you tell someone who has put most of his working life into his property and home that it's time to go? I thought as we sat in the big old club suite in the lounge room. I felt guilty that I'd been the motivator in all of this; and I apologized in advance to Ted and Bernice for becoming so involved in what was clearly their private business. Bernice made the Murphy family's position clear.

"Sweetheart," she said, "without wishing to sound too dramatic, you've been part of this family as long as our own son. Not only do we welcome your comments, but we actually expect them. Ted and I know you have our best interests at heart, the same as Aaron does, so let's listen to what your mum has to say."

We had Mum on FaceTime, explaining the intricacies of the proposal and, importantly, what it would mean for the Murphy family. Aaron and I sat there, mesmerized as Mum drilled down to the most intricate details.

"Now," she said to Ted and Bernice, "take your time to think it through, the three of you, because this is a life-changing decision, not just for you two but Aaron as well, because he owns a third of Carrick."

After a while deep in thought, Ted finally spoke. "Thank you, Sophia, love," he said. "We need to think it all through. I know you'll think me mad, but I feel Trevor all around us at the moment. I've never stopped being Irish, you know. I hope I don't upset you."

"To the contrary, Ted, you and Trevor shared a lovely closeness. I feel comforted rather than upset. It's like he's looking after us."

"I agree."

WE SLEPT in Sunday morning. Bernie had invaded our room, put Sheila outside, and fed a cantankerous Nicky Jr., who was teething.

We finally made our way to the kitchen where Ted was, as usual, using his typically male brain, looking for something that was in plain sight. "You see my Tattslotto ticket, Bernie?" he bellowed.

"Where you put it, *Edward*." She smiled at him. "Pinned to the noticeboard a few millimeters from your nose."

"Oh. Thanks, love," he said.

"Got the numbers?" he addressed the rest of the room.

I read them off my phone, and he nodded his thanks, half asleep.

Aaron grinned at me. His father was not a good riser, while Aaron, Bernie, and I had our body clocks set earlier. There was a funny noise from Ted's direction, as if he was about to sneeze.

"Nick," he said in a peculiar voice, "gimme those numbers again?"

I repeated them with Aaron looking over my shoulder. "You won a prize, Dad?" he asked.

Ted didn't answer, instead he thrust the lottery ticket at us. "Here, fer Christ's sake, check these bloody numbers, will ya? It's a quick pick—that's why I don't know the numbers. But I've won something."

"Dad," Aaron said quietly, "you've six straight numbers, so you've won big money. It was a Megadraw, so you've won two million dollars."

"Break open the whisky," Ted said determinedly. "This deserves a celebration."

"But it's only nine thirty," Bernie said, trying to stir Ted but unable to stop smiling.

"It's yer dad," Ted said, looking at me, "having his say. It's his sign to go ahead with the deal. I know you think I'm mad, but I feel him around me at times, and this is one of them."

Aaron passed him a neat whiskey.

"To Trevor," Ted said, drinking it in two large gulps. He set his glass down and burst into tears, with Bernie hugging him. "We're going back to Ireland for a holiday, darlin', and we'll leave the boys to fix all this stuff."

CHAPTER 62
THE LUCK OF THE IRISH

As USUAL in the Murphy household, mayhem prevailed when Ted was wound up. He sang, drank, and got in the way. Both he and Bernie needed new passports, and I volunteered to take over the process for them. We visited the local Australia Post Office and had their photographs taken.

"Don't we need forms?" Ted asked.

"Yes, but we'll do the online version at home," I replied.

"Oh, you're wonderful, Nick. Why don't we have lunch while we're here. It's nearly midday already."

"I'll drive home, dear," Bernie whispered. "Have a glass of wine with him. He'll go into a coma when we get home, and you can work uninterrupted."

Sure enough, Ted headed immediately to their bedroom, and I got to work. Thankfully, they'd both become Australian citizens and used Australian passports, so it was a simple matter of renewal. Uncle Robert volunteered to be their witness, and the applications were completed in a few hours.

"Tomorrow morning early, it's Australia Post again, Ted," I said. "We'll be leaving at 8:30 a.m."

"Why so bloody early? If we leave later, we could have another nice lunch."

"No."

Ted looked at me quizzically.

"You reckon Dad's up there," I said, "organizing you to win Tattslotto, still a presence in your life?"

"No doubt about it, but it's hard to understand if you're not born Irish."

"Well, I think I do understand, and Dad, as you know, loved a drink. But never before five o'clock. He'd be pissed off if he realized how early you're starting these days."

"But I'm retired now, and I can relax more."

"Ted, you are the kindest, sweetest, most lovely man I know, but if you keep this up, Bernice will be bringing you home to Australia in a body bag. I know you're in training for your relatives in Ireland, but we need you to be around for advice and help as we become fully fledged farmers. Dad would expect that from you."

Ted grinned, no doubt thinking here was a young bloke the same age as his own kid, not suggesting but telling him what to do. "I see yer point, mate," he said, conceding defeat graciously, "but can we have a drink or fifteen after five o'clock?"

"Of course, Dad would be on your shoulder," I said to him as we had a lovely cuddle. There were no years between us. Bernice and I were also like siblings, and Aaron—well, Aaron was amazing. He was strong but gentle with us all. He was the glue that held us together in a most unique family group and business.

MUM ARRIVED in time for an early lunch, having volunteered for airport duty. She was excited for Ted and Bernie. Miraculously, very few people knew of the lotto win, despite Ted's verbosity.

"By the time word does spread—and it will, Ted—you'll be cooling your heels in an Irish winter," Mum said, "away from all the gossips, the charlatans, and the crooks, all looking for a handout."

"Jesus," said Ted, "when do ya reckon it'll be safe to come home?"

We all laughed at him, but it was serious stuff also. "Home is where the hearth is," Mum said. "Where you make it." When they returned, they'd be living in Geelong, an hour away, the link with Carrick forever broken.

Aaron and I have always been on the same wavelength, never more so than at that moment. We smiled at each other as Aaron addressed his father's mindset.

"Your bloody bedroom will be here when you return," he said, "so go and enjoy yourselves."

"Yes," I added, "but you may have to move Nicky Jr. and Sheila out, that's all."

CHAPTER 63
ON OUR OWN

I KNEW I had more to offer than being a bloody housewife. Gay guys invariably had to be multiskilled in a relationship, sometimes switching places as the breadwinner when situations changed. And the changes wrought by Aaron's parents' retirement were fundamental to our life together. Bernie had run the house and helped raise Nicky Jr. to free me up for my business duties in Geelong and on Carrick. Aaron ran the farm, working up to ten hours a day, with Ted following him around, giving sage advice! But Ted, on a good day, was a great worker, so effectively we were at least two people down.

In Geelong, Wayne worked without stopping, so part of my commitment to the family company was to ensure he, Alex, and their kid—or someday, kids—had three weeks holiday.

Each year I would take over their duties in that period, which meant I would be away from home for several days at a time, helping run a student hostel and property development company in Geelong.

Now there were three (four if we counted Sheila), as Mum drove out the gate with Ted and Bernice, on their way to Ireland. Nicky Jr. had to be our number-one priority, but we both agreed he needed interaction with other kids, even though he was too young for kindergarten. We suspected he was advanced for his age and wouldn't be out of place with three-year-old or even four-year-old kids. We knew there were other parents in a similar situation to us from our usual Friday night out at the club, and many of those families lived in our neck of the woods. We did a count and quickly realized most of them wouldn't get a place in the only kindergarten in town, even when they turned three or even four. Nor were there teachers available.

I asked Uncle Robert for help, and he sent us a picture of a portable classroom that Aunt Anne had used sporadically for Sunday School—unkindly but accurately referred to as "Indoctrination Central" by some of the locals. Uncle Robert gave us the classroom and helped install it in its new location on the same block as the current kindergarten. All levels of government objected, but not one resident, so we went ahead with voluntary labor connecting electricity and water. A working bee of local tradies and farmers built a toilet block the following weekend and that too was connected almost immediately.

Uncle Robert was amazing. He spoke to the right people, and we quickly had council building permits and approvals, all backdated.

It was meant to be. Aaron and I were amazed at the seemingly effortless change in attitude of the formerly homophobic schoolmates of ours—David Lane's gang. Only David remained without a partner. The rest had married lovely girls, and they welcomed us into the group. The blokes were wary at first, but when Aaron and I first organized the new kindergarten building then helped with its installation, they appeared gobsmacked!

I winked at Aaron, turned sweetly to the most outspoken of the group, and said in the most seductive voice I could manage, "What's wrong, pet? You expect me to show up in my ball gown and tiara?"

We were part of the mob, meeting usually on Friday nights at the club. The girls would give us a kiss and a cuddle, and I could see their blokes getting restless.

"Where's my kiss," roared out Jack, the most voluble of the lot. Aaron walked over and grabbed him in a bear hug and kissed him passionately.

"Watch the tongue, now," Aaron said. "I didn't know it was that long!"

One could say the quality of the conversation deteriorated after that remark, but the ice was broken. Every Friday the guys fought over who was getting first kiss, and their wives looked on, enjoying the spectacle and watching one of the silliest of Australian customs being abandoned. Generations of men in the past were *never* to show any form of emotion, under any circumstances, according to the very British upbringing of early Australia. While the Williams and Murphy families were raised differently, it was public behavior waiting to be neutralized, and we were the catalyst! Together with Nicky Jr. He squirmed and wriggled in his highchair as his dads were indulging in this "funny" stuff in the club, and he wanted to join in.

He ran to Aaron, holding out his arms. "Tis, tis," he said, so Aaron picked him up and kissed him. But then he held out his little arms again because he wanted kisses from everyone in the room, particularly Jack, who cuddled him up. Aaron decided to have another drink as I was driving, and I heard this purring noise. Our kid had slipped into The Land of Nod in big brawny Jack's arms and was snoring. There were a few damp eyes around the table as our son snored on. He was the star of the show; he had shown unconditional trust, and we were proud of him. We said good night to everyone with our son still fast asleep.

Everything was set except we had no teacher for the new kindergarten. The current teacher was locked in because the ratio of kids to teachers and minders had to be observed, meaning the current kinder couldn't take one more child.

So many things had fallen into place to get us to where we were. I thought the search for a teacher was pointless, but more magic was around the corner—Mum!

She casually asked if we knew of any accommodation in our little town. She had an Indian girl, a newly qualified graduate in kindergarten teaching, who wanted to take up an appointment "...at a new kindergarten down there," Mum said, but couldn't find anywhere to live. Her mother was also looking for work—her husband and the girl's father had been tragically killed in a pedestrian hit-and-run accident recently. I laughed, not believing my ears.

"You shouldn't make fun at another person's misfortune, dear," Mum scolded.

"I'm not, Mum," I said and told her the story of "our" new kindergarten, how for once public servants had obviously got off their derrières and placed a teacher where they were needed. "You remember our shearer's cottage, where Uncle Robert and Danielle stayed for a while?"

"Yes, dear, that's a very nice little place. Why do you ask?"

"They can have it rent free, if they like it. Pay for the utilities only. If her mother is suitable, then we'll employ her full-time as our housekeeper. Award wages of course."

CHAPTER 64
A COMPLICATION

I WAS on the road early; we had a raft of business issues to discuss at the board meeting and some new staff appointments to ratify. Mum couldn't continue to manage the hostel and simultaneously run the family company, that was clear. She was keen to appoint Deepika, the former owner, as her replacement, but Deepika had pissed me off on several occasions. She was very pedestrian in her thinking and could be a bitch, jealous of Mum's achievements, a view I shared with my sister. So, Mum would be overruled, but we had an alternative to offer.

"Danielle," I said to Mum on the car phone. "Alex, Wayne, Aaron, and I agree—she's amazing."

"But dear, she's at university, and there's a lot of study time required."

"Mother of mine," I said, smiling, "since when have any of us worried about eighteen-hour days or doing three jobs at once? Danielle is smart, the boarders love her, and we all reckon she'll be perfect. And a trans person in such a responsible position sends a terrific message to all the community. Don't worry, we won't allow her to fail."

WE WERE nearly halfway when the car phone beeped with a message. My immediate thought was that Mum had messaged me with another item for discussion, so I pulled into a rest area on the side of the highway, parked the old Ford, and turned the engine off so I could read without interruption. Nicky Jr. was fast asleep in his seat as I reached for my phone. It wasn't Mum at all. I felt my fingers tighten around the iPhone because the introduction could only have been written by one person.

Dear Lovely Man, it began. I felt my heart rate increase, and I broke into a sweat in the early morning. But I was curious after all this time. His life-altering behavior toward me had faded away to insignificance, thanks to the Murphy family, and so I read on:

> *You will be most surprised, I think, to hear from me again. Since we parted in Chennai, my good fortune has*

deserted me. My attempt to include you in my household turned all my family against me, including my father. My mother remains on strong medication and is never allowed outside the home without supervision. My marriage was organized by my mother. She was determined for me to marry (as you know), but she didn't research my wife's family properly. After the birth of our daughter, my wife contracted Covid and died two months later because she refused vaccination and treatment. My family have since forgiven me and helped me raise my child so far.

My Lovely Man, you are the only one I love in my life, and I am wondering if you are free to take up our relationship again. I know you will want to get married as many same-sex couples do in Australia, so please consider this a proposal of marriage. Rashid xx

I walked into the dining room and placed Nicky Jr. into his little playpen, which he objected to.

"What's wrong, mate?" I asked, "Wees?" His face erupted into a smile, so we ran off to the big boy's toilet, where he produced a mighty stream. The playpen seemed a no-no, so I put him down in the spare room.

"He'll be awake again right in the middle of our meeting," Mum said.

"I doubt it. He had a shit night because he's teething, and we left early this morning, so he'll be out of it for a couple of hours, I reckon."

Mum studied me like I was a financial report. "And what's up with you, dear?" she said. "Something tells me you're trying to keep a secret at the worst, or perhaps you're simply thinking something over and maybe looking for an opinion from the Steering Committee?"

I laughed at her. It was no accident I'd inherited her sense of humor, and she referred to our current board of directors as the "Steering Committee" when any one of us needed help with making a decision—business or personal.

"I think I might get married," I said with a smile.

"Oh, anyone we know?"

"Yes, I'm sure you'll remember my husband to be."

"That's nice."

"Yes, Mrs. Brown."

CHAPTER 65
THE POWER OF FORGIVENESS

I'D WRITTEN back to Rashid, explaining I was in a relationship with Aaron, and we were planning to get married in a few months.

I am so pleased for you, he replied. *My family told me I was duty bound to offer myself in marriage to you after the harm I caused, hoping we could rekindle our friendship and become partners again. The truth is I have met someone. He is an epidemiologist from the United States, and I will now apply for my working visa there. However, after long discussion with my siblings, I have agreed to present you with a long overdue gift, which although precious to me, will be much more at home in Australia rather than the United States. Are my belongings available? I would understand if you destroyed them, but there are some research papers which would be of great assistance in the future. My best wishes, Rashid.*

I replied to him, assuring him everything he'd left behind had been stored in a container in the barn, but it would need some focus to sort out what he needed. We made a date to meet at the hostel. He piqued my curiosity by asking for Aaron's personal details, explaining it was a gift that required papers to be drawn up and the observation of "proper legalities."

When we turned into the main driveway, there was a hire car parked outside, obviously Rashid's transport. We manhandled a fully awake Nicky Jr. out of the twin cab, and he immediately started calling out to "Gan" and "Danyell," running ahead of us to the kitchen where Mum and Danielle were serving coffee. And some scones fresh out of the oven, the smell of which temporarily took my attention away from the visitors.

Two people. Rashid looking a touch heavier and better for it, and the most beautiful little girl with dark eyes, hair, and beautiful flawless skin. Aaron and I made eye contact—the stunning little creature had to be Rashid's daughter. A loud banging at the screen door turned out to be Sheila; she had pestered us to come for a ride, and now she wanted to see Mum as well. Aaron opened the door, and she flew in, throwing herself theatrically at Mum's feet because she knew a treat awaited those who are clever.

I knew this was my final test. Forgiveness means totally so, not the mild handshake that Rashid offered, but a full-on hug offered by me. He responded, awkwardly because Aaron was there, but relaxed when Aaron pushed me away and hugged him as well. In the back of my mind, I remembered Sam Grover's analysis of my previous mental state, and I quietly rejoiced that I'd found it within myself to forgive, making me a stronger person, but more importantly, done so with Aaron's love and help. We chattered away like three old ladies, Aaron the confident and amazing partner. He knew Rashid offered no threat in any way. A new direction had already been taken, and the hatred had disappeared from the minds of us all.

It was Sheila who drew our attention to other matters. She'd found the little girl, who was fascinated with the attention of her new friend. I couldn't move because I knew how fearful many Indian people were of canines. There are so many stray dogs in India; they can carry disease and if not domesticated they can be quite vicious. Yet here was Sheila, leading the little girl across the room to Nicky Jr. They collapsed in a heap, and Rashid became tearful.

"Look," he said, "they belong together."

Dumb, dumb, dumb. That was me. For someone who had conducted international business deals and helped run a multimillion-dollar agricultural and property development company, when it came to basic facts obvious to other people, I was sometimes a dumbass. Aaron had sensed something, I could tell, but he wasn't saying anything in case he was wrong, and I was disappointed as a result.

"The main purpose of my visit was to apologize for the harm I caused Nick," he said. "This is all I have to offer, the gift I mentioned. I even named her after you. Her name is Nicolette."

Aaron, Mum, and I looked at each other, then burst into uproarious laughter.

"What, what is wrong?" Rashid cried.

Every time the poor bastard asked a question, we just laughed at him harder. Finally, I caught my breath, sat him down at the table, and explained.

"First," I said, "there was Nicholas, Aaron's child through surrogacy, named after me. We now share parenting legally, and we call him Nicky Jr. That's him with Nicolette. Then Alexandra gave birth to a little girl, and she's called Nicole," I said, "so it begins to get a little confusing. Now we have Nicolette, who is also beautiful."

Then the real facts hit Aaron and I, and we held hands.

"Mate," said Aaron, eyeing Rashid, "you want to give away your kid? How can that be? I can't imagine how hard that would be for you."

"I have made the decision based on responsibility, I hope," Rashid said. "I was careless in the past and irresponsible. Now I want to do the correct thing for my child and sign off on the adoption papers." He made eye contact with us both. "I am not doing this because I will be living in America. No, I am doing this because I love Nicolette and want the best life for her. Much better for her to grow up in Australia in a family who will love and care for her. My family, including my father, are adamant she should be here with you, Nick, and your partner. Because I have dual nationality it will be easier than we thought."

"But what about the family back in Chennai?" I asked. "Surely, they would prefer she grows up there?"

"No, they want her here with you because, as you know, they are all very well qualified, and all of them want to emigrate here."

"Yes, she's stayin' here," Aaron's deep voice cut in.

I looked around, and Nicolette had climbed onto Aaron's knee, exploring her new family connection. "But on one condition," Aaron said, smiling. "You need to stay in her life, Rashid. Keeping important information from kids, particularly original parentage, is very wrong because they can feel they've been rejected. She needs to know who her parents were and why she's got three parents now, not just one. We would expect you back here at least once a year, and you can stay at our place. Bring your boyfriend if he lasts the distance."

I winced at Aaron's remark, but Rashid's face broke into a smile. He understood, all right, and was delighted. "Oh, thank you, yes, we will, that is wonderful." He looked questioningly at me, no doubt familiar with me driving the ship as I had done with him.

The fact was that agreement on almost any subject was automatic between Aaron and me. There was no need to check in first.

I nodded my approval, Rashid flew across the room and hugged me, then somehow became entangled with Aaron and Nicolette in a group smooch.

My other half smiled at me. "What about Lettie, short for Nicolette?" he asked.

"Sounds good to me."

CHAPTER 66
A DAY TO REMEMBER

IT STARTED out as early morning drizzle, but by ten o'clock it was pouring, a much-needed rain for this dry, godforsaken place, now edging its way toward becoming a suburb. I was quite comfortable with the weather because the location for the ceremony was right outside the old barn. Wet weather would simply mean we moved into the barn. Both locations, however, shared magnificent views—which for some reason I'd never noticed in the past. I managed a smile as I looked over the hostel and the new houses stretching to the coast, the light towers around the football ground stark in their silent vigil, leaning over as if guarding the home of the Geelong Cats. To our right on the top of the hill stood Max and Val's residence, and past the edge of the building we could see Bass Strait through the gloom.

Perhaps it looks special because it's my wedding day, I thought, laughing out loud.

THEY WERE all there: Bjay and Meera, Dheeya and Sanjay, Ronni and Krish. Rashid's father stayed home in Chennai, caring for his mad missus, and supervising all the grandchildren. They were a splash of color—the girls in beautiful saris, the boys in those smart cotton kurta tunics which looked like pajamas but were just so sensible in warm weather. Aunt Sarika arrived from Mumbai late last night. She was bright, cheerful, yet imposing, inspecting her fellow countrymen and women from Chennai, who seemed a touch intimidated by her gaze.

We gathered in the big dining room for morning coffee; Danielle had been baking, and the cakes and biscuits were amazing. I introduced everyone, making sure the contingent from Chennai felt part of the day, as they most certainly were. Max and Val were there in high spirits, looking wonderful, determined to enjoy themselves. Uncle Robert arrived and was ready to celebrate. He and Ted had become great friends, particularly where a glass of red wine or two was involved. Happily, he'd taken Dad's place in that regard. He and Mum were also closer, the specter of religion no longer hanging over his side of the Williams family. Richard and Amanda were there—both with partners—and Gillian helped Danielle in the kitchen.

"The new normal," Uncle Robert whispered to Mum.

David Canning and Peter were center stage, entertaining everyone, and we'd only served coffee and tea at this early stage.

Oh, watch *this space when David, Uncle Robert, and Ted Murphy get together over a few glasses of shiraz.*

Ted had a peculiar expression on his face as we prepared to walk up toward the barn and the rain ceased as suddenly as if a giant tap had been turned off.

"Trevor," he said with a quivering bottom lip.

The sun came out with surprising force, warming our bones and lifting our spirits. Alex and Wayne's celebrant, Marcia Blackman, was our choice also—she was a lovely person and knew all the tragic twists and turns of our family because she'd been so well briefed by David Canning. She was also totally nonjudgmental, which was helpful in our situation. I looked around the group of family and friends. We'd invited the boarders as well, all of them Indian, and they'd somehow found a version of their national costumes to brighten our day further and to make it a celebration of both South Asian and Australian culture.

Sheila somehow knew it was a special occasion. Bernie had dressed her up in a floral doggy hat fixed to her collar. We told her she looked beautiful, and not once did she try to remove it. She sat with the kids of course; she was never far away from them—Nicole, Nicky Jr., and Nicolette.

We stood up the front with Marcia, and I looked down the hill where the old garage once stood and where the extensions for the hostel had been built, covering up the worst decision I'd ever made. Aaron knew what I was thinking, and he slipped an arm around my left side, followed by the other on the right, and his chin came to rest in the crook between my shoulder blade and my neck, our favorite and most comforting position.

This was very final for us; we'd avoided all the mushy and gushy talk until now, but it was time for us to say to each other what we really thought. I turned in his grasp, looked him in the eye and said, "I love you."

"I love you," he said back, and he kissed me, the effect of which nearly took my breath away. Being Australian and understanding how most Australians loved to heap shit on any show of affection, I expected some ribald and unprintable remarks. It wasn't the case.

Greg, Neville, and their kids had become part of our life and immediately stood up applauding, as did my former doctor, Sam Grover, and his wife. The remainder joined in, including my ex-boss Paul Damon and his lovely Chinese wife, Amy. And my eyes fell upon the couple sitting next to them—Andrew Jones from New Delhi, accompanied by a very handsome-looking Indian gentleman. *A cricketer*, I thought, now standing up and waving in a show of respect and understanding not lost on us. And the others. Our mad mates from home, with their kids. Our newest friends: tradies, farmers, stockmen, their partners and kids. Standing there for us, cheering even, clearly well lubricated, and determined we knew they loved us.

How amazing is this new Australia, I thought, and Aaron squeezed my hand. He knew what I was thinking, as usual.

The ceremony was simple yet rather memorable due to Marcia and her interpersonal skills, which kept our guests and us on the same page. We signed the papers at a nice little table then posed for photographs with our children.

It was not only a new beginning, but perhaps a continuation. We had two kids to raise, a farm, and a property-development business to run, along with Mum, Wayne, and Alex. Finally, I'd begun to think plurally again; not me, but us.

A *gentle man* and me, together, plus kids.

Continue reading for an excerpt from
The Eleventh Commandment
by John Terry Moore

CHAPTER 1
IN THE BEGINNING

MY FATHER, an Irishman, styled himself as the unequivocal head of our household, and he didn't care if he broke the Ten Commandments because he was the boss. He ruled the roost, and no one dared defy him, not even God himself.

My first memory of anything was my father yelling at me. I was only a little bloke, about six years old. I had a younger sister, Mia, and our little brother, Timmy, was a newborn. I'd gone to Mum, who was feeding him. She finished and showed me how to burp him. I was so pleased I'd done something right. I really loved Timmy. He looked so cute as I cuddled him. He grinned at me, so I leaned in and kissed him before handing him back to Mum.

"Benjamin, you fuckin' little poofter." Dad's voice came from the doorway. "Boys are supposed to be men. Ya don't kiss other boys!" he screamed. He knocked me off the chair onto the floor, and I cried with the shock and the pain of it. It was the first time anyone had hit me. Mum screamed back at him, but the old man laughed at her. "I'll raise these kids to be men, not pansies. Real men don't kiss other men."

There were similar instances as I grew older. I somehow survived because of what the old man made me—an arsehole like him. His behavior drove Mum and me closer, and while I resisted his upbringing, I suppose a certain amount of conditioning took place over which I had no control.

CHAPTER 2
COLLEGE—AN EDUCATION IN LIFE

I LIKED gay people. Many of them had a struggle with their families, like I had, but for different reasons. The gay kids I met in college had mostly been damaged in one way or another in the process of coming out, and I was a straight boy brought up in a household with a violent father. I think I originally became friends with gay guys deliberately to antagonize Dad. He was a beer-swilling, foul-mouthed fuckhead who hated "poofters" as a matter of principle. "When you have a name like O'Connor, you have to fight for yer rights," he said. "A man can't even have a peaceful drink without some do-gooder or poof havin' something to say about it. And what's more, these Chinks, Indians, and all these Muslims need blowin' away. They'd steal the food off yer table, even take the beer outta ya fridge, and that's serious."

My gay mate Kenny Ho wanted to meet Dad "to see if people like him really exist" or whether I was exaggerating. His eyes nearly fell out of his head when I introduced him one Friday night. Dad and his fucktard mates were in the garage, half of which had been converted into his playroom. There were green streamers hanging everywhere from the roof; St. Patrick's Day was a few days away, and they were working up to it.

"You wanna drink, sissy boy?" Dad asked Kenny.

"Oh, I'll have a soft drink, thank you, Mr. O'Connor."

"A soft drink."

"I'll have the same, Dad," I said, trying to make Kenny feel better.

"Listen, real men drink beer or whisky. There's none of that other shit here. By the way, where do you come from?" The room fell silent for once, and I thought here it comes, the full-on racial taunts were about to start. I thought perhaps we shouldn't hang around much longer when Kenny took over.

"I'm Australian, Mr. O'Connor," he said with a note of pride. "Fourth generation actually. My family originally came from China. We're immigrants, like your family, Mr. O'Connor, but I think our mob's been here a little longer than yours. Thanks for your hospitality. Enjoy St. Patrick's Day."

I couldn't contain myself; I giggled uncontrollably as we walked outside. Dad had been cut off at the pass so decisively he was lost for words. I grabbed a change of clothes before he went completely crazy. Mum had agreed I could have a weekend with Kenny and his family. Anything sounded better than Dad on the warpath.

As it turned out, that was the beginning of my real education. We greeted Kenny's parents, then walked past them to the stairs. Kenny reigned supreme on the top floor. He was an only child and had his every whim catered for. Mumsie and Daddypoos left him alone, never questioned him at all unless his academic performance faltered. He was a brilliant kid, and he was smart enough to study when he had to.

I'd been sexually active with several girls, but when Kenny got me home and offered to blow me, I accepted. This time it wasn't to upset Dad. This time it was for me. I was sick to death of chicks who wanted to "go steady" and others who were deliberately trying to trap guys so they could be trophy wives with a four bedroom brick veneer and a German car in the driveway. He really knew what he was doing, wrapping his lips around my dick and taking me to heaven. I glanced casually at him as he really got into it but freaked when he dropped his own trousers.

"I'm not gay, Kenny. You know that, don't you?" I said.

"Who cares?" Kenny grinned. He was a really good-looking bloke, quite well-built and rather stockier than most Asian guys. "Listen, we're having fun. My guess is you're not even bi. The chicks are all over you like a rash, and you do have a reputation for sticking your dick in everyone who says yes."

I laughed at him. He was a crazy guy, and we were great mates, but I'd allowed my sex drive and my curiosity to get the better of me. Not that I was complaining. It was true that guys gave better head than chicks. At least Kenny did.

But it did worry me a little—because underneath it all, I really enjoyed this shit.

CHAPTER 3
MUM

As it turns out, Mum has been the only woman I've ever loved.

Dad's alcoholism got worse, and a few weeks after my hookup with Kenny, it all came to a head. His mongrel mates left for the night, and he stormed in the back door, yelling for his dinner, forgetting Mum was working night shift at the hospital after leaving a plate for him to microwave. He screamed for Mia to look after him. "Women were put on this earth to make sure the menfolk don't have to cook their own fucking meal," he roared and punched open her door to find the room empty. Next was Timmy's door, with the same result. He thought he'd be cunning in my case, opening my door quietly, but it didn't work because I was already outside shepherding my sister and brother over the fence to Mrs. Donaldson next door. Lorna Donaldson was a gem, she did housework for Mum, cash in hand, and was the only human being to whom Dad showed any fear. She made us cups of Milo and fed us with fruitcake, which calmed us down, helping us forget the tirade of ugliness from our father, who we could still hear yelling at no one next door.

The lights from Mum's car reflected in Mrs. Donaldson's kitchen window as she swung into our driveway, and I sprang out of my chair and hit the ground running. I had a feeling something bad was about to happen; Dad was the worst I'd ever seen him, and Mum was about to walk into a shitstorm.

I made it to the kitchen door as my father swung a punch at Mum's head. I flew in between them and hit him in the stomach as hard as I could, winding him, his fist connecting with Mum but most of the power gone. A flash lit up the room as Mrs. Donaldson recorded the moment on her iPhone, with my siblings looking on, terrified. Mum sank to her knees, sobbing both with pain and the realization that her marriage was over. Dad stumbled to his feet and charged toward me as the flashing blue lights of the cops filled the house and feet ran along the veranda, while Lorna Donaldson bravely recorded every moment.

The cops had Dad in handcuffs before he could do any more damage, but the noise level didn't drop—it increased. The look on Mum's face said it all; Dad was intent on waking the street so all the gossipy neighbors could witness her shame, trying to hurt her as much as possible, physically and mentally. The three of us kids ran over and hugged her, desperately trying to stop her pain—probably not succeeding, but at least she knew we loved her.

She straightened up, pointing to the kitchen table, and we sat down, Mrs. Donaldson joining us. "Thank you so much, Lorna," Mum said, "for keeping them safe. If you hadn't been here, goodness knows what may have happened."

"We're a good team, missus."

CHAPTER 4
STRUGGLE

MUM GOT me to the end of that college year, but it was obvious I couldn't go to university even if I wanted to. Mia and Timmy needed to get their VCE, so it was my turn now to take on the world and help Mum. She had help from Centrelink, and her nursing salary paid the mortgage, but we had to eat, and her savings were running out. She'd bought Dad's share of the house, and with the help of a friendly bank manager, which is a rarity, she refinanced it. Dad eventually declared himself bankrupt in his business as a builder, and Mum saw almost nothing toward the upkeep of Mia and Timmy. She worked long hours for modest wages, Mia worked in a day care center as a helper, while Timmy was the best little housekeeper ever! He could (and still does) create nice meals out of nothing. I shadowed the big supermarkets, even began working in one near home so I could have access to the free chuck-outs of food, which found their way straight to our table in many cases. The old expression "hand to mouth" was never more appropriate than in our case.

I cursed my old man for his lack of interest and total absence of financial support, but Mum and I agreed our independence was worth much more than the potential of more violence in the kids' lives. I was a tough prick. Nothing the old man could say or do scared me in the slightest, and I managed to tell him so every time I ran into him. Constant conditioning had forced me to live up to his adage. "The world is full of cunts," he'd said. "The only way to survive is to be a bigger cunt than they are."

It hadn't worked for my father, but I knew I had to be tough as I struggled to make a living for our family. I was quite handy with mechanical things, and I was given a really good heavy-duty rotary mower by an aged neighbor with no further use for it, as he was moving to assisted living. O'Connor Home Maintenance kept me busy during daylight hours, and I worked at Woolworths on the evening shift, stocking shelves.

I was sweating my guts out one day on a vacant block of land behind my new mower when this smartly dressed dude waved me over.

"Yeah," I said, "what do you want?"

"Why don't you turn that fucking thing off so we can talk," he yelled.

He looked familiar, and I thought he might be from a local real estate agency. He was youngish, maybe in his early thirties, and seemed intent on holding up progress—my progress.

"You from the real estate people?" I asked.

"I'm the owner, Andrew Smithson."

I remembered him now. He was one of the upwardly mobile young Turks around town, his perfect features everywhere on the internet and the newspaper, probably making squillions out of real-estate sales in a boom that seemed to go on forever. I read everything I could lay my hands on when I had time. I knew somehow my family would beat the poverty cycle and I could move on to something a bit easier. So I tried to keep up with what was going on around me in lieu of a university education.

"I've been watching you," he said, a smile on his perfect face.

"You want my body or something?" I snarled at him.

He roared with laughter. "You'd need to clean yourself up first." He smirked. "No, I came to offer you a job."

"What as," I said as forcefully as I could, "fucking office boy so you can hand me around?"

"Oooh, you do have a chip on your shoulder, and you're desperate, aren't you, working nights at Woolies to feed your mum and siblings and to educate them? But there is an easier way."

I knew he was deliberately winding me up, so I went all sugary sweet on him and pretended I was interested. He quoted a figure as a base salary that was more than I earned in a month, plus a percentage of each sale that would make your head spin.

"Why me?" I said, amazed.

"Several reasons. Like I said, you're desperate. You're also a hard worker, and you're an arsehole like me. You'll do well. I've got two people on staff at the moment who're fucking lazy, and I've put pressure on them. I know they'll both go on to other agencies eventually. By the time they're gone, you should be producing, so the opportunity's there. You got any decent clothes?"

"Only a funeral suit."

To my astonishment he peeled a thousand dollars off a wad of notes and handed it to me. "Go and get a decent suit and shirts, properly fitted, shoes and everything, a modern haircut, and your nails done. Give all your personal details to Gloria at this number. I expect you at work next Monday."

CHAPTER 5
SMITHSON REAL ESTATE

I REFUSED to allow the family to wind me up; they were ecstatic for me and seemed to think we'd go from rags to riches overnight. I knew there are really no freebies in life and working for this prick meant I shouldn't get ahead of myself. But I did allow Mum to fuss over me. She'd earned the right to dream a little, to come home and begin to enjoy her life again. She was leaving no stone unturned and decided I needed a consultant to look me over—Kenny.

"Gay men know how to dress," Mum said, "and they have a sense of style. Kenny is so beautiful. I'll bet some of it will rub off on you."

We hadn't seen much of each other lately, but he was still one of my best mates and could be relied on. He brought another guy with him, complete with enough hairdressing stuff to open a new salon at our place. They commandeered the dining room, and the results were spectacular. I could hardly recognize my own ugly self in the mirror.

"Okay," Kenny said, "thank you, Julian, we'll be in touch." He instructed me to pay Julian, who stood there, a silly look on his face, as I handed him his money. "Ben needs to shower now, and I'll finish the styling, thank you."

When I came out of the shower, Kenny dropped to his knees and blew me as if it was all part of the normal service. Thank Christ it was Saturday and everyone was out. I actually felt relaxed for the first time since this madness had begun. Kenny styled and gelled my hair and showed me how to look after it.

"What about your license?" he asked.

"What about it? I still have one."

"Not your driver's license, your real-estate license. You'll need that to operate."

"Fuck, I didn't know about that."

"Look, I think they accelerate the process with new people, but I downloaded the forms necessary. Let's fill them out together."

My new boss was blown away. To have a newbie front up on the first day with his license application filled out was unheard-of. "Unfortunately, you have to do some study before you'll need this," he said seriously, "but we'll fast-track you as much as possible. In the meantime, I want you to be my shadow. Watch me, and if you don't understand anything, ask, right?"

I nodded, aware I had much to learn.

Gloria was Andrew's PA, a bosomy fortysomething chick who looked me over like I was this week's sacrificial lamb. I wondered if I'd have to throw her the odd fuck to get anywhere in the future, but in the meantime, I homed in on her as the best source of information on how the place ran, who was up who, and how the industry worked.

To my utter surprise, Gloria was a very nice person, which certainly didn't fit in with my new boss's lack of character. Nor did it fit the real-estate image as a whole, at least my perception of it. She was enthusiastic to a fault and explained the paper trail and legal requirements in the first few days. I discovered that she held a license herself and could fill in for any of the salespeople in a flash. It took me a few days, but I finally worked out what motivated her—money, pure and simple. Yes, she probably loved a bit of cock, but that was quite secondary to earning a dollar. She drove her "baby," an aged Mercedes sedan with a big V8 engine and totally inappropriate in today's energy-focused world. But she liked nice things, and besides, every time she turned the key I think she got her jollies. I made a mental note not to get anywhere near the driver's seat; it was probably permanently damp.

My boss, Andrew, reckoned I was a quick learner. "Listings drive the business. If we don't have anything to sell, we might as well close up shop. It's a matter of getting to the seller first. Drop everything and get there fast." He looked at me with a crooked grin on his film-star face a few weeks into my "cadetship." "Run this scenario through your mind," he said. "You have your homework done on the way, as we discussed, you know the prices other properties are bringing in the immediate area, and Mr. and Mrs. Fuckwit want a ludicrous amount no cunt in their right mind would pay for what's probably a heap of shit, needs paint, repairs, and throwing half their junk out to make it look bigger. So, what would you do?"

"Agree with them," I said. "Sign them up at their price and get sole agency for at least sixty days. Then when it doesn't sell, blame the market and get their asking price back where it should've been in the first place. From day one, work out what turns them on. If the little woman takes a fancy, string her along, make her your best friend. Tell her she looks twenty years younger than she really is and she'll eat out of your hand. Or maybe it's hubby who fancies a bit of rogering on the side. Tell him he's hot, admire his fucking vegetable garden or whatever else turns him on, but use him to retain this business."

Andrew looked at me in sheer admiration, a smile on his handsome face. "But I want you to think about this: you have the potential to ruin my business, ruin me and yourself to the point we could never work in this town again, if you don't honor the Eleventh Commandment."

"What the fuck's that?"

"Think of the Ten Commandments, then add one more—Thou Shalt Not Get Caught."

Scan the QR code below to order.

JOHN TERRY MOORE hails originally from Tasmania, the Australian island state. He completed his education at Hobart Matriculation College, was a farmer and Tasmanian champion single sculler for several years, runner-up in the Australian competition.

After coming out to his family, John made his home in Victoria, holding a number of senior positions in the Victorian automotive industry over a thirty-five-year period. Subsequently, he became a civil marriage and funeral celebrant for many years (now retired), witnessing firsthand rapidly changing Australian public opinion, questioning traditional family structures and culminating in the marriage equality legislation passing into law in December 2017.

He married his partner Russell Baum on February 21st. 2018.

However, John remains concerned that the fight is never over; right wing politicians, together with some church leaders would seek to wind back the clock to the bad old days where the scourge of homophobia was a major cause of suicide in men under thirty years of age.

Consequently, John seeks to normalize same-sex relationships and inclusiveness through his writing, encouraging all young people to live their lives truthfully, fearlessly, and with dignity, as is their right.

John's interest in economics, politics, and Asian affairs has also played a major role in his writing, and he is unfazed in taking on contemporary issues, including the scourge of coronavirus.

John and his husband have traveled extensively throughout Asia, inserting themselves into the culture and the daily lifestyles of the local people, and consequently have a unique overview and a deep understanding of Asian and South Asian nations, which also feature in his writing.

John and his husband, Russell Baum, live in Geelong, Victoria's largest regional center, one hour from Melbourne, Australia. They were flower growers, raised stud sheep, and bred Kelpies, Australia's working dogs, before moving to Wandana Heights, a Geelong suburb, in semiretirement.

There they have a large network of friends, mostly with canine interests in common. John collects clocks when time permits and fervently espouses the health benefits of red wine.

A
Nice Normal
Family

JOHN TERRY MOORE

Jackson "Jacko" Smith is dyslexic, but like many people affected by the learning disability, he is highly intelligent. His best friend Sammy Collins helps him get through school and unlocks his potential. Jacko progresses through the ranks of local government until Mother Nature intervenes and the straight boy and the gay boy become a couple.

As Jacko and Sammy start a family and challenge social mores, Jacko enters politics, horrified at the direction the Australian government is taking. With Sammy by his side, he can achieve anything and rises through the ranks to the highest office in the land, driving Australia away from its British colonial roots and engaging with its neighbors in Asia like never before. Economic growth results, and while most Australians are supportive, a small group of extremists might endanger everything Jacko has built—including his life.

Through the love and the strength of their partnership, Jacko and Sammy rise above their ordinary lives. Because love is never ordinary.

Scan the QR code below to order.

BLACK DOG

JOHN TERRY MOORE

Australia is a nation in transition. Marriage equality looms but homophobia still rules. Depression and suicide are commonplace as Dean Prentice and his lover, Danny, grow up together in country Victoria. When Dean moves to a nearby regional center to study veterinary science, he finds acceptance and love when reunited with Danny. Profound tragedy visits Dean's life and he grieves, moving on through a series of lovers both male and female and struggling to focus on his studies and his dream of becoming a veterinarian. He graduates and specializes in equine work.

With long hours and unrelenting pressure, he misses the support of a full time partner. The only constant in his life is his loyal Kelpie, Bruce. Then he meets Neil Andrews and falls in love. Neil is a stunning widower in his forties with children and grandchildren, and Dean realizes he wants kids of his own.

But Neil is still deep in the closet and while their relationship is passionate, it's going nowhere permanent. They separate, and Dean contemplates marrying a woman for company and friendship. For the second time in Dean's young life, depression reveals its ugly presence; this time there are medical professionals at hand and he might have a chance for love at last.

Scan the QR code below to order.

For more
great fiction
from

DSP PUBLICATIONS

visit us online.
WWW.DSPPUBLICATIONS.COM